MW00413486

A Gangsta's Pledge 2

By: EL Griffin

Nyasia (Nya)

When I woke up, the first thing I felt was a pounding ass headache and pain in my face. I reached my hand up and cringed. My face was swollen and the slightest touch from my fingers felt like a hammer pounding down. It felt worse now than when the nigga was throwing the blows to my head back to back.

I tried to open my eyes slowly. Little by little, fighting past the pain. But even with my eyes open as far as they would go I was only looking though little ass slits. Making everything appear smaller.

Whoever attacked me, just left me in the same spot from the looks of it. Laying on my back, looking straight up, the blue sky and the bright ass sun almost blinded me. Since the sun was almost directly overhead, that meant I had been out here for hours unconscious.

What the hell happened to Saint?...

I got to the hotel just after midnight and now it seemed like the middle of the damn day. After they shot into his hotel room

6

and dragged me away, I prayed over and over for him to be okay.

Maybe he wasn't coming to the door when I knocked. Maybe he made it out and didn't know to come look for me.

Worry and panic set in and gave me the motivation I needed to get my ass up. I could never give up on my fucking heart and that's what Saint was to me. I didn't have time to feel sorry for myself. I needed to fight through the pain I felt and find out what the fuck happened to him. Fuck everything else.

I struggled to sit up, taking small breaks between movements to catch my breath. My ribs were all fucked up from my attackers too. There was a soreness between my legs, from being raped. Memories of the first time I was raped at my aunt's came back for a quick second before I pushed them aside just like the pain.

I caught my breath, sitting in the leaned up position against the dumpster for a few minutes, regaining enough strength to stand to my feet. I held my side where the sharp pains shot through my body. Walking slowly step by step, staggering forward. I made my way to the busy street at the end of the alley.

I didn't have a phone or any of my shit that was in the bag I brought for the trip. Who the hell knew where the bag was now.

7

So my best bet was to go back in the hotel and get somebody to tell me what happened to Saint.

People began to notice me as they walked past on the sidewalk, sending me crazy ass looks. But none of their asses tried to help or said shit to me.

After turning and walking around the side of the hotel, I found the entrance and walked through the automatic doors. Once I stepped inside, the receptionist came running over to me. Then lent me her arm for support, just about holding me up.

She was an older lady probably in her fifties with a sincere look in her eyes. Even through the pain, I noticed the soft worry lines etched on her caramel complexion. Her face was like an angel to me right now.

"Thank you." I managed to whisper the best I could through the sharp pains that came with each breath.

"Oh my! Call an ambulance!" She yelled out louder than seemed possible for her.

"What's this about?" Some younger woman coming out from the back asked, looking between me and the lady who came to my assistance.

"She's hurt and she needs to get to the hospital now!"

"Calm down and keep your voice lower. Stop being so dramatic", the rude ass bitch said with an attitude. She even rolled her eyes.

I swear if I wasn't in so much pain I would have popped her in that smart ass mouth. Her evil ass didn't give fuck about my condition, but that disrespectful shit was what had me wanting to fight the girl. She was being all extra treating this woman like shit for no damn reason. I hated bitches like her.

"I will not calm down. But I will tell you, you better call 911 yourself, or you can bet your ass, you'll be fired and lose that manager position behind a lawsuit." She responded back with just as much fury as I felt.

I had to give it to the woman she really was my guardian angel right now. Standing up for me the way she was. In that moment I was indebted to this woman, whoever she was.

"Hurry up...." I heard her voice fade as my vision blurred then went black completely, losing consciousness again.

Jolie

A week had passed since I got the worst phone call of my life telling me that my brother was shot up and in the hospital here in Houston. I was too hysterical to make the flight and get out here on my own. Thank God, I had Buck by my side to help me keep it together. I needed to be strong for my brother, just like he had been strong for me my whole life.

Buck was almost as fucked up behind this shit as I was. He never even was the type to give a fuck, but this shit had him barely sleeping and his temper was at an all-time high. Especially when it came to the hospital staff.

For the first few hours we didn't have a clue where Nya was at. A small part of me even questioned if she was behind this shit. I knew her ass was supposed to come out to Houston and surprise Saint the night he was shot. Now all the sudden she was nowhere to be found and up and disappeared without a trace.

The other part of me, prayed that nothing bad happened to her either. It was just as possible that the niggas responsible for this shit got a hold of her.

While we were waiting on an update about Saint, one of the nurses told us that another person connected to the incident was being brought in. I stood by as they wheeled my best friend to the back feeling fucked up that I ever doubted her in the first place.

Nya wasn't even recognizable. Her face was so messed up. It looked like the men who did this used her as a damn punching bag. I held her hand while she was taken to the back. I didn't even want to let go when the doctors and nurses insisted that I leave. Finally Buck pulled me back so they could do their work. But I still stayed right there with her the whole time.

That was a week ago. Nya recovered just fine and now was gonna be released from the hospital later today. She still had a bruised up face and her ribs still had a while to go before they were healed all the way, but she was okay. For that I was beyond grateful.

Now as far as my brother, he was still touch and go between critical and stable condition.

Saint suffered multiple gun shot wounds, being hit four times. One in the abdomen, one in the leg and another in the shoulder. The worst one was the bullet to the neck. He lost so much blood from that wound that the doctor's didn't know if he would ever wake up from the coma he was in.

I had done more praying in the last week than in my whole life. I felt that my brother wasn't going no damn where, that it wasn't his time yet. He was too strong, too much of a fighter to let some bullshit like this take him out. If anyone could come up out of this, it was his stubborn ass.

"Come on, let me take your ass out to eat. You gotta get out of here for a while." Buck came up behind me, wrapping his arms around me from the back and holding me close, as he entered the hospital room.

"Okay bae, but let me wait 'til Nya gets here. She's supposed to be here in a few minutes. They're bringing her in here after she signs the release papers. You know her ass ain't going nowhere without Saint.' I answered Buck.

I wasn't about to let my brother sit up here alone. Buck had one of their workers posted in the hallway by his room, but I still didn't want to leave him alone in case he woke up.

He deserved somebody to be by his side when he woke up and know that he could count on us for that shit. I had to give it to my girl too, she was solid as fuck when it came to Saint.

Here she was recovering herself, still making it a priority to stay by Saint's side as much as the staff let her.

Now that she was being released, she already let the whole hospital staff know she really wasn't going nowhere. Her ass was stubborn as hell like my brother was, so I didn't doubt that she meant exactly what the hell she said.

About a half hour later Nya came into the room, walking nice and slow. She was getting better each day and the bruising in her face was almost entirely gone. Her dark complexion covered up most of the discoloration, but the swelling was a different story altogether. When she first came in her entire face looked like a balloon, she could barely even open her eyes.

It was a blessing that both my best friend and brother made it to the hospital alive. This shit could have been a whole lot worse with neither of them left alive. Now, I just needed Saint to wake his ass up and then things could get back to normal.

Buck and Saint's crew out here in Houston were supposed to be on the lookout for whoever was responsible for this shit. But with the two of them still being new to the area and the team under them not even becoming acquainted with their bosses yet, it wasn't looking too good for finding them anytime soon. At least not until Saint woke up.

All Nya said about the shit, was that there were three men. I felt like she was holding something back, because when she told me about what happened and everything she remember she wouldn't look me in the eyes. NyAsia Miller was as honest as they come, but even when we were kids, if she tried to lie she would avoid eye contact.

So I knew her ass knew more than she was willing to let on. I would let Saint get to the bottom of everything once his ass woke up. Best believe he wasn't gonna go for the okie-dokie shit she was giving either.

"Okay girl, we're 'bout to go grab something to eat. You want something?" I asked Nya after she came in the room and checked for changes to Saint's condition.

Unfortunately, there wasn't any changes to report. The nurse would be making her rounds in another hour so I needed to make it back in time. The only way they gave you any damn information was if you stayed on their asses. My brother wasn't about to be getting any half ass care in this place.

"Where you going?"

"We're just gonna stop by that same spot from last night, Nicey's. Their shit is fire. You gotta try something. I swear it's amazing."

"Alright, just get me whatever you get. Thanks." Nya responded in a sad voice. This shit with my brother was really waring on her.

Even though I was stressed and worried, I wasn't the type to stay down. I always tried to stay positive to get through difficult shit. The love my best friend had for my big brother was so apparent, that I knew he was in good hands when I left. The love she had for him, was the real deal.

It was like the love I felt for Buck. The shit ran as deep as possible. The kind of love where the other person becomes your family. Shit, they become like yourself. You love them the same as you love your damn self. That was some real ass love shit.

I patted her on the shoulder and leaned down to give her a quick hug before following behind Buck out of the room.

I hated everything about hospitals. From the stale ass air, cold rooms and rude ass people. I just hoped my brother got up out of here sooner rather than later.

Buck and me were basically out in the open with our relationship now, the only problem was that he didn't come clean to Saint before he was shot. I was relieved that my man finally was stepping up and showing me love, claiming me for the world to see. But I knew there was gonna be some shit behind it when Saint woke up.

That was another thing I hoped and prayed would be settled quickly, right along with Saint's recovery. Buck was going all the way out, taking care of me showing me how much he loved my ass. I appreciated everything he was doing.

He walked behind me over to the passenger door and leaned forward brushing against me, then stood back up. He turned me around and gave me a juicy kiss, then slapped my ass.

"Get yo' ass in the car shawty. Wearing shit like that gon' get you fucked up. " He said referring to the sundress I had on.

Niggas loved when women wore dresses. And I only wore thongs, so my home grown fat ass was free to bounce more with every step I took. I knew that my man loved to watch my ass when I wore them. I smiled at him giving him the look he loved so much right back. I was ready to fuck just as much as he was.

Since being out in Houston we hadn't had sex. But now that Nya was released and my brother's condition had stabilized more, it was time to relieve some stress. I needed some dick that only my nigga could give me.

I sat down in the passenger seat and took my time looking at Buck. He was just so damn good looking. He was double my size and full of muscle. His hair had grown out some, along with beard. He was hands down the finest man and he was all mine. My pussy got wetter the longer I stared at him.

All of the sudden, Buck slammed his hand against the top of my head pushing it down hard. Shots rang out close as hell and glass came crashing down on top of me.

"Ahhhhhhhh." I screamed and ducked down even further into the seat.

I closed my eyes and tried to remain calm. Just as fast as the bullets came spewing in the car, the sounds abruptly stopped. I heard tires screech and a car speed off, so I sat up fast as hell trying to see who did this shit.

The front windshield was shot completely out and whoever did this was already gone. I turned my head to check on Buck and lost my fucking mind.

"Oh MY GOD!!!! NO, NO, NO. Wake up!!!!! Buck!!! Baby wake up."

I reached over and pressed my hand over his chest. Blood seeped out covering his T-shirt and my hand.

Tears poured down my face. This couldn't be happening. I tried to get Buck to respond. I put more pressure on the hole in his chest and continued to call his name, trying to get him to wake up.

"HELP!!!!!!!!!!!!" I screamed.

But it was too late. He had no pulse, no breath. He didn't answer. He didn't wake up. No matter how much I shook him, called his name, kissed him, there was nothing.

Nya

As soon as Jolie came in screaming and I saw the gurney wheeling Buck away, I ran over to where she was. I grabbed ahold of her and forced her back, holding her in a hug.

She cried, screamed, tried to get past me to follow where they were taking his body, and all I could do was hold her. Finally Jolies' legs gave out and she dropped to her knees on the floor.

"He can't be gone! He can't! Oh my god, why? I can't..." She cried out with short breaths from hyperventilating.

I didn't have shit to say that would make her feel better. Buck was gone. In the blink of an eye, everything changed and he wasn't here anymore. After a few minutes, Jolie quieted down and cried silently with her hands covering her face, chest heaving still on her knees.

I had to get her out of here, but I couldn't leave Saint either. I was at a loss as to what to do. So instead, I dropped down to my knees right next to her. Fuck it, if she needed to cry and get this shit out, then I was gonna be right here by her side.

A few tears fell from my eyes along with her. Buck was a part of our circle. Our small family that we created.

I couldn't believe that one minute he was up talking, joking around. Finally being out in the open with his relationship with Jolie, and the next, his body was being wheeled into the hospital in a body bag.

This shit was too much of a coincidence. My head was telling me that this was done on purpose and connected to the same shit that happened to me and Saint.

I thought back to the night I had been trying to forget, and replayed the words the nigga spewed at me before he knocked me out. The only thing he said was that he "found me".

"ME"... All of this shit was because of something in my past. I already felt sick behind Saint being shot and in a coma because of me. But knowing that Buck might've lost his life behind some shit that was meant for me, made me feel like it would've been better if I never came back to New Orleans in the first place.

Was all of this shit my fault?

I hadn't told Jolie about what the man said either. I wanted to wait until Saint woke up and let him handle it how he saw fit. It seemed like the best thing to do since it might have to do with my past and I wasn't ready to face that shit yet. Saint was the only one who knew about my life in Houston, stripping, and how bad I was living.

But me not saying some shit may have just cost one of my best friends his life. Buck didn't do a damn thing to deserve that. Street niggas lived knowing any day could be their last day, but that was because the choices they made. If this was because of me, his blood was on my hands alone.

I wiped away my tears. Saint needed to wake the fuck up. I held the guilt in and continued to comfort Jolie. We stayed on the floor for another few minutes. When her breathing and crying slowed down, I helped her stand back up.

"What happened?" I finally asked.

"I don't know. One minute we were talking, kissing, then the next.... Oh my God Nya, he saved my life! He pushed my head down. He died because he was more worried about me then himself... I can't go on without him, I just can't!"

"I know girl, but that man loved you more than anything. You're gon' get through this shit. I know it hurts. We'll get through this together. I love you."

"Love you too." She answered leaning in for another hug.

A cough from behind us caught both of our attention. We turned in the direction the noise came from. I expected to find Terrell checking on us to see how we were.

He caught the flight out here with Jolie and Buck to be with me while I recovered. My little brother tried his best to be my protector even though it wasn't his job. At 17, he tried to play the big brother role whenever he thought I needed him to.

But instead of seeing Terrell, we were approached by some random nigga walking over to us. Me and Jolie stepped apart and glared in the direction of the man who was being rude as fuck, interrupting us. Right now anyone could get it, was how I felt.

My first thought was maybe he was the police or some shit, trying to see if we had information about what happened. No matter what the fuck happened, the fucking cops were the last people we would talk to.

After getting a closer look, I knew that the man in front of me didn't have shit to do with the police. He had a cocky ass demeanor and his suit looked way more expensive than the cheap shit even the best detective could afford.

Before I got a chance to see what the first man wanted, Drew, came around the corner. He looked stressed the fuck out. But he was holding it together.

Drew and Buck were pretty close and he was in the hall when they brought him in.

He walked up to the man in front of us and nodded his head in greeting showing respect.

Shit, if he knew who the man was and didn't warn him away, maybe he was here for a reason. Drew was the only white man on Saint's whole damn team. He was the only person period that we had right now to count on for shit. Saint vouched for him and let him get close. That shit said a lot about what type of man Drew must be, because Saint didn't trust hardly anyone.

Drew had been keeping Buck informed with all the business dealings out here since Saint was hit. He was the one making sure that Saint's room was protected. His attitude was one of a street boss just like Saint's and Buck's but he was humble with the shit and didn't overstep.

I had never seen a white boy so confident and cool with it. Some people were just built for this lifestyle and it definitely suited him. He was even sexy for a white boy.

But trustworthy or not, he was slipping letting Buck get shot out in the open in the middle of the fucking day. I was gonna let his ass know that shit whether this man was here or not. I might not be his boss, but I didn't give a fuck when it came to the people I loved.

"How this shit happen? I thought you were taking care of things?" I said in a cold voice looking directly at him. I didn't give a fuck who the other man was. I needed some kind of answer as to why and how Buck got hit.

"We only got one man on the door to Saint's room. That was on Buck's order. He didn't want to pull anyone else away from the streets. You know him and Saint don't do that security shit on themselves." He said shaking his head.

Jolie started crying again, then went and sat down in one of the window seats against the wall. I could tell Drew was hurt behind the shit that happened. Him and Buck seemed to be pretty cool, especially since Buck didn't even talk to mothafuckas.

He was right, I couldn't even argue. Saint told me when I first got back, that him and Buck stayed under the radar and didn't need a team of niggas around them. That they could handle their own shit.

That mentality just cost Buck his life. Always being so fucking hard headed. I shook my head right along with Drew.

I finally turned my attention to the other man standing next to Drew. My guard was up. He looked at me and Jolie like he knew exactly who we were. I was good at reading people but this nigga, was unreadable.

He stood with a straight face. He was about the same height and build as Saint, milk chocolate complexion and chiseled out features.

"Who's this?" I asked Drew.

Instead of Drew answering, the nigga spoke up for himself, "I'm Juan, I'm Saint's brother."

That caught Jolie's attention and she responded to the man, "Why are you here? Ya'll ain't got shit to do with each other." She spat out nastily.

Damn, it seemed like there was some family shit that I didn't know about. A part of me felt funny that Saint kept some important shit from me. Maybe it was some shit that came up when I was gone and that was why I didn't know.

I liked to think I knew everything about Saint, because I felt like he knew all about me. But the truth was, we still had a lot of catching up to do before he was shot. I didn't open up about any of the shit that happened to me when I moved to Houston, so I had no reason to feel left out, as petty as it was.

"He called me about a month ago. We've been in contact since." He answered still not showing any emotion in his voice.

I was able to tell that he had the same no bullshit attitude that Saint did. He spoke his mind and got straight to the point, like

25

my man. Maybe it was an inherited trait or maybe I missed hearing my nigga's voice too much.

I intervened, because my best friend wasn't in the right mind and the last thing she needed was to put up with some unnecessary bullshit.

"Why are you here?" I asked.

"We set some shit up. I'm here to get him the fuck outa dodge and make sure he's taken care of while he recovers." The nigga said like he ran shit.

I noticed he had a slight accent.

"How do we know you're telling the truth? That you're who you say you are and that we should trust you with any fucking thing." I said back bossing up on his ass.

He might've thought we were just two typical timid women. But he had it twisted if he thought just because Jolie was upset crying that we were gonna let him tell us what the fuck to do. Trying to take saint any fucking where like he was talking about doing.

"Jolie knows who I am... Me and my brother ain't close, but if I say some shit, it's what the fuck I say it is." He answered looking at Jolie.

She turned and looked at me nodding her head one time, letting me know the shit he was saying was the truth. All I could do was go with what this nigga I had never met before was saying, I guess. But that didn't mean I trusted his ass one bit.

"So what's the plan?" I asked.

"He's got too many enemies here, I'm having him moved to my home in Puerto Rico. Nobody can know except the people standing here now and your brother, he said referring to Terrell.

I've already made arrangements for his medical transport. Everything's taken care of. You and the family are supposed to travel tonight on my private jet." He said as if reciting a well thought out plan.

"I'm not going nowhere with you. I'm not leaving Buck. This is all some bullshit!" Jolie raised her voice, answering Juan.

I needed to keep my cool. Right now we had to do what was best for everyone. I looked the man in his eyes and finally saw some type of emotion. He looked sincere. I stared his ass down and then turned back to Jolie. He better be 100 percent honest with this shit.

"Honey, we'll have Buck sent to New Orleans and come back for his home going at the end of the week. We got to do what Saint would want...You know him better than anyone" I said gently to Jolie calming her back down.

She continued to cry and finally shook her head in agreement.

I didn't check to see or get an okay about the funeral arrangements, but one of my friends had just been shot and killed, my best friend was heartbroken about to lose it, and the man I loved more than myself was in a coma. No matter what, I was gonna do everything in my power to handle shit the right way.

I needed to be strong and hold shit down until Saint could come back to us. I was gonna be the woman he needed me to be, the one he knew I always was before I even knew it myself.

His ass had to come back to us because we all needed him more than ever now.

Tonya

"Fuck me, YESSS, just like that!!" I coached the nigga I was fucking while he dug in pussy from the back.

"Stop talking hoe and take the dick then."

He slapped me on the ass hard. Fucking with this nigga was turning out to be more fun than I thought. Having a common enemy in that bitch Nya only made the sex better.

Watching the way he was taking care of shit and fucking with her life was almost better than any orgasm I'd ever had. At least he had a good size dick that touched my stomach when he gave deep strokes. His ass liked all that rough shit just like me, making our sessions even better.

Everything was coming together. It was only a matter of time before me and Saint would be reunited just like I planned. The only shit that hadn't gone the way I wanted was my sister losing her life.

The injuries she suffered at Saint's hotel room left her dead on scene before the paramedics arrived. I couldn't be mad at anyone other than that bitch Nya.

If she never came along and distracted Saint, there would've been no reason for me to set shit in motion with the nigga I was dealing with now. He may have pulled the trigger, but Nya was to blame for trying to take what was already mine.

Even with the fucked up shit I did to my sister, at the end of the day she was still my sister. A part of me loved her. I knew my faults and that I was selfish. But fuck it, that was how God made me.

I still loved her as much as I could. She was the only person who ever really cared about me or showed me unconditional love. She was someone I counted on to have my back no matter what.

I was sad behind the shit and the way her life had to end. My little niece or nephew died that night too. She was pregnant by Saint's ass and planning to tell him the same night she was gunned down, according to the diary I found at her apartment. She really was in love with his ass. But didn't know a damn thing about his real life.

She was such a fool behind that nigga. That was why she was dead now. That shit couldn't have been me. I might be doing the most to claim the man but that was because he had the things I wanted. Big pockets, real power and the best damn dick I ever had. His fine ass could get it any time he wanted.

Regardless of all the shit with my sister, I was still determined to make Saint mine. I never gave up when it came to what I wanted. This nigga I was fucking with was good and all, but my eyes were set on Kwame "Saint" Harris.

In the process, I was gonna get some kind of revenge for my sister. She deserved that much. That bitch Nya hadn't felt nothing yet according to what was in store for her.

"Bitch, stop fuckin' moving!" He grabbed my waist and squeezed tight. Locking me in place.

I did just like he said and completely froze in place, letting him take control of my body.

"Fuck, ssss, aaaaahhh." I moaned enjoying the deep thrusts he threw at me.

I started grinding my hips nice and slow, popping my ass in an even rhythm. This shit drove all the niggas crazy. His ass was no different. He moved both hands on my ass and started pumping faster fucking my insides up.

I clenched my pussy muscles and let it rain down on his dick, squirting on the mothafucka. His dick pulsed and got harder inside me, letting me know he was about to cum.

I pulled away, letting his dick to slide most of the way out. Then looked back over my shoulder. I started twerking my ass making it clap just on the tip of his dick, while he jacked the base. His cum shot out all over my ass and down my back.

I crawled over to the edge of the bed and stood up gathering my clothes to get dressed. It was time to get the fuck back on my grind and come up with my next move with Saint. Laying up with this nigga wasn't an option. Fucking was all either of us wanted, and now it was time for me to bounce.

After hooking up with Julius this morning, I ended up coming back to my Aunt Renae's house. I needed to get my mind right and figure shit out. Her ass was home like always, but I went straight to the room I was staying in, instead of making an effort to talk to her ass.

I laid down on my bed, turned on my Spotify playlist and pulled some Cush out to roll a blunt. I needed to get my mind right.

Shit needed to happen faster. Right now, Saint was in a coma and there was no telling how long it would take for him to wake up. I had snuck into the hospital and tried to visit him one time this past week, but he was gone.

It had only been a couple weeks since he was shot and his friend's funeral was last week. There was no way Saint just woke up and left without a trace in such a short amount of time. Or maybe he did.

Wherever the fuck he was, I needed to stay as close as possible to Julius. He was in the streets heavy enough to hear if his name came up. He already had a team of niggas on the lookout for him. Or that was what he told me anyway. I didn't trust any nigga alive for shit. So now it was time for me to make some moves on my own.

For the time being, I was stuck staying with my Aunt. This was the first time we had actually ever lived under the same roof and I was seeing a whole other side to her.

The setup she had and the shit she was into, even struck a nerve with me and I had a lot of fucked up ways. She let her nigga pimp out young ass girls in her home. She didn't just go along with the shit, she was hands on pimping them right along with his ass.

Hoeing was the one thing that left a bad taste in my mouth. My mama ended up walking the street when she couldn't pay rent and I hated all the random niggas she brought home. But to each their own, it wasn't none of my business at the end of the day.

My funds were low and now that Toya was dead, I had to deal with the shit for a little while longer. I was confident that by the end of the week some of the regular niggas I used to fuck with would be financing me again. Most niggas were gullible as fuck. With some sweet talk and good pussy, they would forgive me for leaving them high and dry, like it never happened.

At least my aunt gave me my own room. Even if the shit was small as hell it was clean. That was one thing I could say about her, she kept a clean ass house. The shit was a one story brick house that sat on a decent street in a middle class black neighborhood. Not exactly the suburbs outside of Houston, but a step above the hood and ten steps above the projects I grew up in as a kid.

"Hey bitch, what you got going on later?" My aunt poked her head in my room and asked.

I continued to vibe out to the song playing, "Booed Up". This was my shit and it was the song I dedicated to me and Saint's situation. When the song ended, I answered her.

"Damn, can't a bitch get some privacy?" I answered, only half joking.

"Not up in MY Gotdamn house you can't! Shit, I pay for this shit. So when I ask, I want an answer right away not 5 fucking minutes later with your stuck up ass."

"My bad, I'm just trying to figure shit out right now"

So far I hadn't told my aunt about the shit I was into. But I did give her Saint's name to see if she knew who he was. She said she never heard the name "Saint". But after running it by her nigga, the name did turn out to ring bells in Htown.

That was how I ended up meeting Julius. It was my aunt's boyfriend's brother. It really was a small ass world. Now this man I linked up with, Julius, knew exactly who Saint was. He had some kind of vendetta against him.

We were supposed to work together, but he was trying to cut me out of the fucking loop. He wanted to get rid of Saint and his bitch. All I needed was Nya's ass gone, and my man safe and sound.

I wanted Julius to help me get information until I could deal with Nya, then I would get rid of his ass too. That way it would be me on Saint's arm. I could help him get over the loss of the bitch he thought he loved so much.

Maybe my aunt could help me get rid of Nya. I didn't have anybody else to turn to at this point. She always bragged about being the bitch that handled shit with these hoes she had around here. Now it was time for her to put her fucking money where her mouth was. I hoped she knew a way to get rid of a person quick and without anyone else finding out.

"Can I ask you a question...?" She gave me a blank stare so I kept talking. "I know you're a down ass bitch and that you know all the ins and outs of this street shit. I don't know nothing like what you've been livin'. I see how you handle your business and I'm trying to learn the best I can from you, but I ain't got time on this one. This shit is serious."

I worked her ass the same way I did niggas. I built up their ego to get something I wanted.

I paused then hit her with what I wanted, after seeing she bought every word I fed her.

"Do you know how to make a bitch disappear?" I asked in a nice voice this time showing all the fake ass respect I didn't feel.

I needed to be on my aunt's good side. Maybe she really could help me with this shit and it would be lights out for Nya. My aunt could help me get a gun and she had a car. With her help I could make shit pop off.

She started nodding her head, with a big ass smile plastered on her face. Yup, I had her ass.

"What do you want to know?"

Nya

A month ago we laid Buck to rest. Me and Jolie set up a private burial and service for him. The only people in attendance were me, Jolie and Drew. The hurt was still hard to deal with for me, but for Jolie it was consuming her. I tried my best to be there for her and help her, but sometimes time is the only thing that will ease the pain. She was really going through it right now.

There was nothing worse than the finality that came with losing a loved one. When someone dies it changes everything. Shit just would never be the same again. I could only imagine how Saint was gonna deal with finding out his best friend was gone.

Drew stepped up and proved that Saint was right to trust him more than the other mothafucka's he had working for him. Even with shit coming crashing down, Saint in a coma, then Buck getting hit, Drew still kept the operation in Houston moving forward.

He was the one who planned everything for the service for Buck since we were in Puerto Rico. Most other people would have saw this time as an opportunity to advance their own position and say "fuck" Saint.

That was what happened back in New Orleans. Drew broke the news to me and Jolie yesterday. As far as the streets knew,

39

Saint and Buck just up and disappeared. Nobody had a damn clue as to what happened or where we were besides our small circle and the niggas that did the shit.

Back in New Orleans, Smoke took it upon himself to step up and become the unofficial boss in their absence. That nigga was trying to holla at me being real disrespectful was a sign of the shit to come. He was just waiting for an opportunity to come against his supposed to be homeboys. More than that, they were the niggas who looked out for him and made sure his pockets were filled. He proved to be the grimiest type of nigga.

From what Drew said, Smoke told their team that Saint and Buck were both dead and he was the next in line based on what they would want. Whoever wasn't with it was put out on their asses. He was too much of pussy to even take out his competition for real. His stupid ass didn't even seem capable of running shit from the few times I was around him.

I just hoped my man would come up out of this damn coma. The sooner the better. I was over all this waiting and hiding.

Staying in Puerto Rico was okay for the most part. I mean it was beautiful out here. We were living a life of luxury. It turned out that this side of Saint's family was into black market smuggling on some real shit all around the world.

So far Juan had kept his word. But I didn't trust but a few people and that shit wasn't gonna change in a matter of a month. So far so good, but who knew when or if he would switch up. There had to be a reason that Saint wasn't close to the nigga to begin with. That stayed in the back of my mind at all times.

Puerto Rico was going through a lot of changes right now since the hurricane last year, so all me and Jolie did was basically stay at the villa. Terrell was adjusting to the change just fine. He was trying to holla at one of Juan's daughters who was around the same age.

Juan even came to me about the shit, but I let him know there wasn't gonna be no problems with my brother. They were just kids and even if he was trying to get close to the girl, he wouldn't be disrespectful to his home or letting us stay with him. I raised him better than that shit and already had the talk with him. There was no mixing business with pleasure.

The problem was Terrell's ass needed to be back home, in school living the life of a regular ass teenager. Not on the run, hiding out because I was dating a street boss. I really needed to do better by him and give him some security once this was all over with. That shit was gonna be one of the first things I talked to Saint about when he got better.

I still wasn't doubting him coming back to us. It was just a matter of time in my mind and my heart.

Juan's home was large and beautiful beyond our wildest expectations. Saint's family was wealthy as hell. Beyond that new rich shit. I could tell that they had been about this shit for generations from the property and the respect the staff gave them.

But no matter how good it was here, me and Jolie both were in a funk. We didn't even do much talking these days outside of the necessary. My girl was hurting and I wasn't a whole person anymore without my other half. It was like all we did was watch the clock waiting for Saint to wake up.

"I want to sit with him for a while" Jolie said coming into Saint's room.

Lately she had been having a real funny ass attitude. It was only directed at me, so I knew there was more to the shit.

"Okaaay. You want me to leave or something?" I asked.

I mean, I knew she was hurting but that didn't excuse disrespect from anybody, even my best friend.

42

"Damn, can't I get some time with MY brother?"

I raised my eyebrows and tilted my head to the side. Did I hear her ass right!

"Wooooaaaah, you better calm all that down. I know you're hurting and losing Buck is fucking with you, but I'm still the same Nya. Still your best friend. Your damn sister. So what's really good?" I asked.

I really wanted to know what the hell was up. Jolie was usually the peacemaker in any situation. She was the calm, collected and happy girl. She could bust heads, but only when she needed to. This shit wasn't like her.

"You suppose to be my sister and your keeping something from me?! That shit is funny as hell...What? You thought I couldn't tell that you knew more than you were telling me! I know your ass Nya, and you ain't been honest about the attack to begin with. Let me find out you're the reason Buck's dead and my brother is laid the fuck up in a fucking coma! I will kill your ass myself, fuck all that talking. Matter of fact, don't speak on Buck again or see what the fuck happens." She screamed at my ass and stood in my face toe to toe ready to fight.

She must have saw the look of surprise and then probably the one of guilt. But it wasn't what she thought. I was withholding some shit, but I still didn't know who the fuck did this. I didn't mean for anything to happen to anyone. Tears welled in my eyes, but I held that shit back. My best friend was coming at me and I couldn't say a damn thing to defend myself.

We could fight it out and really fuck some shit up, but I couldn't even be mad at how she felt. I blamed myself every fucking day for what happened to Saint and Buck. I didn't' mean for nothing from my past to hurt the people I loved.

I wasn't trying to intentionally hide shit from her in the beginning either. It was just easier to avoid talking about my life before. I didn't know that Buck was gonna get shot.

I backed up a few steps and looked away over in the direction of where Saint was laying in his hospital bed.

"It ain't even like that... I was just waiting for Saint." I said quietly. I wasn't a quiet person, but I couldn't even argue with her. Maybe this was all my fault.

"Well as you can see, he ain't waking up right now. So you better explain some shit right fucking now!"

I raised my head and looked at her ready to explain that it was a man, a voice I didn't recognize that said "he found me". It was the only thing I knew about who it was.

But before I could, the machines hooked up to Saint began ringing loud and fast as hell.

When I looked back in his direction, Saint's eyes were wide open, locked on mine. All the blood drained from my face and I felt light-headed. I held my hand over my mouth and cried. Tears of joy fell from my eyes for the first time ever.

Saint

Imagine hearing yelling and screaming, startling you up out of a deep, peaceful sleep. Waking up just to feel excruciating pain and watch the two women you love arguing by your bedside. That shit was fucked up. They were doing way too much at the wrong fucking time and place.

I knew I had been in a coma. I heard Jolie and Nya talking sometimes. I kept trying to come up out of the darkness and the dream filled sleep, but I just couldn't open my damn eyes. Then when Nya and Jolie were going at it, something in me clicked and I finally was able to wake the fuck up.

Trying to pull the shit out of my throat hurt like hell, but I couldn't talk or do shit with the mothafucka restricting me. Nya and Jolie stopped their argument and hurried over to my bedside. That's where their asses should have been instead of the bullshit they were on.

"Wait! Don't touch that, wait" Jolie tried to tell me.

This respirator shit was gonna hurt whether the doctor's took it out or I did. I would rather be in control of it then them.

"Slow down bae, wait for the nurse." Nya added right behind her.

Fuck that. I continued to pull the long ass tube out of my throat. I didn't need to wait for shit. It did make me cough bad as fuck and gag a few times. But I got the bitch out.

I signaled for Nya to give me a drink of the water sitting on the tray at the foot of the bed. She caught on to what I wanted and held the cup up to my mouth for me to get a drink.

"What the hell ya'll doing arguing and shit when a nigga's on his deathbed." I said trying to ease the tension between them. Talking was harder than I thought and I had to talk slow as hell.

Jolie glared at Nya and gave her a look, like she was telling her to start saying something. Shit was off. I needed to hear what the fuck Nya had to say, because from Jolie's expression I wasn't gonna like it.

Nya hesitated. She looked down and then back up before our eyes met. Yeah, I wasn't gonna like this shit at all. I could read my woman up and down like a damn book.

"Say what the fuck you got to say." I had been in a coma for who knows how long. I didn't want to waste any more time.

"The man who shot up your room, well the men. They took me to an alley... and when... well he said something about "finding ME". I didn't say anything about it and was

47

gonna wait until you woke up to run the shit by you. I didn't want to involve more people. But then Buck... and it's all just fucked up. I'm sorry. I'm so sorry for everything." She said between tears as she told me what happened.

"What the fuck they do to you? And what happened to Buck?"

"They...they beat me pretty bad and you know...." Her voice trailed off.

"They touched you, my fucking wife. They violated you!" I said angry as fuck.

No mothafucka should have come close to touching Nya and that was what the fuck she was telling me happened. I saw why Jolie was tripping and that the niggas had said they "found her". Meaning Nya was the reason I was shot.

But it was still my responsibility as her nigga and the boss I was, to protect her and make sure nothing happened to her. Shit, in my eyes it was my responsibility before we were together. She was my family. So this shit was on me, not her.

I sat up more, ready to get out of this mothafucka. I had major moves to make.

"Don't worry 'bout me, I'm good." She said way too causally for me.

"Fuck all that shit you're talking. You ain't good. Look at me." She lifted her head and her gaze met mine again. "I got you. I love you, you heard meh"

I said I loved her for the first time ever, reaching my good arm out and wrapping it around her waist.

My body screamed out in pain, but I set the pain aside and tried to comfort Nya the best I could. I loved this girl more than anything. Thinking about the shit they did brought out feelings I had never felt before. I never wanted her to hurt or go through nothing like this.

She leaned in and kissed me on the cheek, but I wasn't going for that weak shit either. My dick was already brick hard. My sister was in the room and I needed to get out of this bed first, but Nya's ass was gonna at least give me a real ass kiss. I turned my head and gave her a deep kiss.

"Okay, damn bro. I know your ass got some hot ass breath, and doing all that" Jolie said sounding happier than what she just was. Then she looked at Nya and her eyes turned cold again. I picked up on all that shit.

"What else?" I asked. I was smart I knew there was some more shit.

"Buck got shot... He didn't make it." Nya said with sorrow in her voice.

"That's right tell him how because of you my man is gone. How his best friend's gone. You still gonna talk all that love shit knowing what she cost us?!" Jolie said right back angry.

"Hold the fuck up. Your man? The fuck that mean?" I asked. I really wanted to know what the hell she was talking about.

"We were gonna tell you, but then this happened... I'm sorry. But we loved each other Saint. You gotta believe that Buck was gonna come to you. He just ran out of time and now he's gone" Jolie sputtered realizing she was caught up.

I was fucked up behind losing my partna. My nigga didn't deserve to die so young. I couldn't even imagine being in the streets conducting business without my fucking nigga. We were brothers through and through and best believe I was gonna get some kind of retribution for this shit.

But if I was understanding right, my sister and best friend had been hiding a whole fucking relationship for a while now from me. Who knows how long they were moving behind my back. That was fucked up in a whole lot of ways. He broke the fucking code. The more I sat thinking about the shit, the madder I was getting.

I felt betrayed by both of them. My sister was my sister and she kept all her personal shit from me. But my nigga had violated by even fucking with my sister and

50

then not telling me about the shit was some real snake shit. It was a straight up betrayal. I guess I couldn't' even trust Buck's ass even after all these years.

"Get out. I'll talk to you later. But right now, get the fuck out of my room. This shit ain't what I'm trying to hear right now. My sister and my best friend fucking around behind my back. Lying to my fucking face. Now my nigga's dead and I don't even know how to feel about the shit."

I said causing my throat to dry back, making me cough. Damn it was gonna take some time to get my voice back to normal.

Right now I wanted my sister to get out of my face with the fuck shit she was on. She looked at me in disbelief, but then turned to walk out of the room. She gave Nya one last dirty look before she made it out.

Right now I needed to get to the bottom of who was behind the hit and who the niggas were. I needed to get up out of wherever the fuck I was and start getting some answers. The only person on my team that I could even halfway trust was Drew.

It was time to hit the streets hard and make mothafucka's pay. Blood would be spilled. Wasn't no way, any of the pussy ass niggas behind this were getting away with the shit. I bet that on everything.

Nya

I was still waiting for Jolie to come to her senses and talk to me. Here it was 2 months after Buck was laid to rest and she hadn't said shit else to me, not one time, since the day Saint woke up. I didn't even know that shit was possible.

If you would have told me my best friend would end up hating me, I would have thought there was no way. But as the days continued to go by and she continued to shut me out of her life, I was more convinced that she really didn't care about me or our friendship.

I still hoped eventually Jolie would be able to forgive me for whatever she thought I did. The fucked up part was, none of us could really move on until we got to the bottom of who was responsible for what happened. It was a clear planned out hit with a team of niggas involved. But so far Saint wasn't able to get much information.

It didn't help that he didn't have the pull he used to right now in the streets. After he woke up from the coma he spent a little over 3 more weeks recovering in Puerto Rico, getting his strength back up. Being laid up in a bed caused him to lose a lot of weight. But he was slowly gaining it all back again in muscle from his daily workouts.

We hadn't had sex yet either and that was just about killing him. I used to be able to go without fucking for as long as I wanted to. But since he turned my body out I wanted the dick as bad as he wanted some pussy. But until his new doctor gave him the green light then I wasn't about to risk his health no matter what.

He was at an appointment now. This was his first one since being back in the States. We flew in yesterday to New Orleans and were staying on the outskirts of the city in a small ass motel.

Saint didn't even has his ID on him and was determined not to show his face around town yet. He wanted to take Smoke by surprise. All the fallout from this shit was so frustrating to him. He vowed to make sure he had things in order for the next time.

I kept reminding him, that there needed to not be a "next time", but his ass wouldn't stop reminding me that anything could happened to a street nigga. He was mad as hell and feeling like a failure for thinking he was so prepared for any damn thing, except what the hell actually ended up happening.

To me, Saint just needed to relax and give himself a break. There was no way to plan for every damn thing. This was all unexpected and it really was on me anyway.

He was already getting to work on taking his shit back and was supposed to meet up with the Uptown boss later today. Ron was the nigga who ran uptown and the same nigga I knew since childhood. Saint was meeting with him on the strength of me vouching for him when we were talking about his next move last week. He didn't trust people, but I mentioned how Ron used to be a family friend to my parents.

Saint never had problems with the uptown crew or anybody from around that way. They weren't exactly friends, but he told me about their business agreement and how everything had been sweet up until this point. I believed Ron was still the same boy I knew back in the day and that he would ride this shit out with Saint.

He had enough gun power and clout to help him get his damn position back, it was just whether he was gonna stick his neck out or not. Saint still technically had his operation out in Houston, but that whole setup was still vulnerable since he just took over a few months ago. He didn't want to involve any part of his business out there with what was happening back home. Luckily, Drew was still holding down shit in the meantime.

I did leave out the part about how Ron used to try to convince me to be his girl, or that he was my first kiss. That shit was so long ago and never went that deep for me. It was just a childhood crush on his part.

Who knew if Ron was actually gonna be solid on this shit or whether he was gonna do some snake shit himself. Me and Saint talked about that possibility too. But being that Smoke was running his organization and the word was he had gotten rid of all of Saint's loyal men over the past month, he had to do some desperate shit to get an inside option as to what to do next.

It was fucked up to think that in a matter of two months everything Saint worked hard as hell for over the last decade was swiped away from him. That some greedy ass nigga on his team would go against the grain. Coming at him in his one weak moment, after years of Saint of breaking bread with him.

Saint even told me about how he planned to get rid of Smoke for the shit he pulled with me. That was before any of this shit went down. But he didn't make it a priority and was waiting to find out more information about how deep the plot went. Now it had come back to bite him in the ass.

Saint was confiding in me more and more these days. Really trusting me and even asking for my opinion on shit. I wanted to be everything he needed me to be and then some. He was my everything, so anything I could do to help, I would do for him.

Hearing him say "he loved me", made everything that much more real for me. Now Saint was telling people I was his wife and just all the way out there for me. I would do absolutely anything for the nigga I loved.

"You ready?" I asked coming back into the small motel room, seeing that Saint was back from his appointment.

I didn't mind staying at such a small ass place. This was the type of shit I was used to before coming back home. Now Saint was different story. He felt out of place and could hardly sit still the couple of days we had been here. I was just glad that the place was clean. Fuck the size and cost. I didn't need much. As long as Saint was good and we were together I was content with wherever the fuck we were.

"Come here." He called to me from the edge of the king size bed where he was perched.

I obediently walked over to him and stood between his legs, like I loved to do. This was the only time I felt in control and dominate over Saint. When I was standing between his legs, close, looking down into his eyes. The first time I admitted my feelings for him and got close to him I was standing just like I was now.

"The doc said I'm good shawty." He wrapped his arms around me resting his strong hands on my ass, pulling me into him.

His face was right by my pussy, turning me on. Being so close, knowing I could finally get some dick that I had been waiting for. But we had to leave if we were gonna be on time to the meeting.

"Uh, uh. I got you later. But right now, we go to go if we're gonna be on time."

"Fuck all that. Take your clothes off and put that pussy on my face." He said then slapped me on the ass.

Shit, fuck the meeting for now. My nigga wanted to eat my pussy. His mouth, juicy lips and tongue were a close second behind getting dicked down properly. The way he looked at me turned my insides out and made my knees weak in anticipation. Damn. I wasn't about to turn this shit down.

"Yes daddy." I answered. My pussy missed the feeling of his tongue and his dick.

Saint laid back on the bed, with his legs still hanging over the side.

I was dressed in a burgundy halter sundress with only a bra and thong underneath. I lifted the form fitting dress up over my head and threw it on the floor, then took the rest of my garments off until I was standing nude.

I got on top of my man and straddled him, leaning down and giving him a deep sensual kiss. My breasts pressed against his chest. The coolness from his gold chains on top of his shirt made my nipples even more sensitive causing me to let out a slight moan.

I wanted to show and make him feel how much I loved him with the kiss. This man was my heart, and I wanted him to know that no matter what, no matter how bad his trust was fucked up, I wasn't going nowhere.

Growing impatient, Saint broke the kiss and grabbed me by the waist, lifting me straight up. He did just the fuck what he wanted with me and eased me down on his face. My pussy directly over his mouth, and dove in.

He circled his tongue around my entrance, then moved to my clit. He put it right between his lips and sucked nice and slow adding pressure.

My body started tingling, the heat building in my core. Saint was driving me crazy. Making my body want more and something hard to fill me. But he just continued to suck and flick his tongue faster over my clit.

He was straight up playing with me, not giving me what I wanted. So I began riding his face pressing my pussy on that mothafuckin' mouth of his, letting my nigga really go to work. I popped my pussy moving up and down.

My moans got louder and my body tensed up in response. I reached my hand down behind me and found what I was looking for. Saint's dick was rock solid trying to get free. I began stroking his dick through his pants to the rhythm of his tongue moving back and forth.

I went faster with Saint's mouth movements matching my pace. He was alternating between flicking his tongue and sucking on my hard clit. He lowered his hands and palmed my ass with a tight grip before latching the fuck on my clit, not letting up.

When he did that shit, I came down hard and tried to raised up to release my cum and let my orgasm go, but I couldn't. Saint knew just what the fuck he was doing and that I was about to cum and instead of letting me move away, he held me in place. He stopped sucking on my clit and slid his tongue inside me.

Saint was eating my pussy so good that I couldn't even form a thought. The nigga was killing my shit with his tongue acting like my cum was his favorite meal. My juices gushed out, with his tongue still buried in my pussy. He kept sucking and slurping until every drop was in his mouth.

Finally, he lifted me up off of his face. My body was so damn weak that when he let me up, I fell over to the side not able to move. I never had a nigga eat my pussy before Saint and the shit he just did took my damn soul.

After a few minutes my breathing calmed down and when I looked up I stared at Saint completely naked standing on the side of the bed stroking his dick, looking down at me with a gleam in his eyes. Damn he was sexy as fuck.

"You ready."

"I can't move yet bae... but I want some dick." I said honestly. I was still fucked up behind the way he just ate me out.

"Nah you're ready, Fuck that. I'm bout to kill the pussy shawty. I know your ass ain't tapping out" He challenged.

His ass was on a mission to leave a mark. But fuck it, my body would just have to recover later. The longer I looked at his big ass dick, sexy body, and the man I loved, the more ready I was to take the damn punishment.

He reached out and grabbed my ankles pulling me over to the side of the bed where he was. When he got me to the edge he flipped me around, so that I was on my knees. I arched my back and made my ass toot up in the air.

SMACK! "That's what the fuck I'm talking about. My ass shook from the impact and I clenched my pussy from the excitement it caused. Then he slapped my ass again, harder. I dug my hands into the bed cover taking the pain and pleasure it caused, racking through my body.

Saint used his hand and gripped the back of my neck, then pressed my head down into the mattress, making my body bend all the way over and my ass to come up more. He was on that straight dominant shit right now and I was for it all.

"Your body's perfect, damn your pussy's fat."

He rubbed my ass hard easing some of the tenderness from the slaps he just landed. Then he took his hand and began fingering me from behind. My body responded right away and my juices could be heard against his hand as he worked his fingers in and out fast.

Then Saint stuck his finger in my ass and continued to work his fingers in and out of both of my holes.

Being filled completely gave me a new pressure I had never felt before. I moved slowly with his hand. My nipples were hard as hell, rubbing against the bed making them more sensitive.

"Oh my god, Yes, fuck." I screamed out, before everything tightened up. My breathing stopped and I cummed again. The wetness dripped down my leg soaking the mattress. Before Saint, I never got so wet, now his ass caused me to squirt.

Saint let me get everything out and pulled back from working his hand in my pussy. He turned me around and slid his dick in nice and easy. His demeanor switched up and he began taking his time with me.

His dick hit the base of my pussy pushing against my fucking stomach. He started sucking on my nipples giving each one attention. He gave deep strokes moving in a circular motion, with his dick fucking up my insides each time. This was some other shit.

"What're you doing to me?!" I managed to get out between strokes.

He continued to slow stroke me looking me in the eyes. I tried to pick up the pace, to relieve some of the pressure and fuck him back. But this nigga refused to go faster. He kept digging in deep and fucking me up with the motion he was putting on me.

"I love you shawty, you my rida for life, my wife." He said part by part between moving in and out of me. His dick rubbed right on my clit and he finally let me move enough to wrap my legs around his torso.

"I love you too!" I moaned with tears in my eyes.

He was making love to me, like I had never been made love to. He was doing everything to me that I had never experienced. I loved Kwame "Saint" Harris more than a person should love someone else. I just hoped he didn't make me regret it. I was gonna let him in. All the way in, finally.

Saint

This was some fucked up shit, but I
didn't have nobody to blame but myself for
losing control of my own damn team. All
because I wanted to wait shit out and not go
off my instincts and get rid of Smoke from the
beginning.

Now I was out here, staying at a
fucking motel and shit. Most people would
think I could just go up in my house or
businesses and get the shit I needed, but it
wasn't so simple.

With Smoke being in charge of the
West Bank, the moment I stepped foot over
the bridge there would be a target on my
back. My brother Juan had informed me of
the shift of power back home before we
landed in the states. Drew already brought
that shit to me, but if Juan knew, then it was
known to every mothafucka in the
underground circles we moved in.

I was tempted to say fuck it and go in
alone with Drew as my backup. I doubted
most the niggas who were working for him
would come against me, when I was the real
fucking boss.

The operation in Houston was mine too
and I could have some niggas out here in no
time. I thought about going to my restaurant
or strip club and picking up some heat and

money to make shit a whole lot easier too. I had plenty of options.

But, all of them would put me at a disadvantage somehow. Either by making my team weaker or scaring Smoke away before I got to his ass. This fuck nigga had to go. I didn't want to chance him running off and it be another lose end. Then his bitch ass would go in hiding and I would be stuck looking over my shoulder like I was already having to do behind this other shit in Htown.

I knew Smoke wasn't the nigga behind the shit in Houston. He didn't know enough about the city and only went with me out there that one time at the end of the takeover. Even then I didn't fill him in on any of the details. Whoever did the shit was familiar as hell with the location for how smooth it played out on their end.

That didn't mean Smoke didn't know about the shit. The reason I even left his ass breathing after I peeped that snake shit with Nya was because I wanted to see who else he was scheming with. Now I didn't give a fuck and wasn't waiting for shit. He was a dead man walking.

Me and Nya were using the funds from her account that I set up. I had her pull out a few hundred when we landed in the city. That way mothafuckas couldn't trace our location now. I was paranoid before with just the police after my ass. Now I had to watch for all the mothafuckin' snakes around me that I couldn't even see.

Jolie had her ID and credit cards, bank cards and shit. I told her ass to stay in Baton Rouge for the time being. But other than that I hadn't said shit else to her. As long as she was safe and out of harm's way that was all that mattered. She knew how to stay under the radar if needed. She was smart as hell, but right now I really wasn't fucking with her.

She called the burner phone Juan gave me every damn day, leaving messages begging me to talk to her. She pleaded her case over and over about how she loved me and was sorry for being with Buck behind my back.

I was gonna forgive her. Shit, I already did, but right now I needed to keep my head straight and get my mothafucking organization back. Shit needed to be settled on top of finding the other niggas that needed to fucking die.

Without having my funds and niggas behind me, I wasn't shit out here besides a bum ass nigga. I couldn't do a damn thing but take what the fuck happened to me like a bitch. I wasn't planning to stay down another damn day.

The meeting with this nigga Ron was supposed to help me figure out the best way to get rid of Smoke and take back control of my own fucking team. I just hoped he wasn't on no fuck shit and this wasn't a set up. He was the only nigga in town that knew I was back. My damn girl was the one who put in the phone call to the nigga to test the waters on it.

I didn't like that shit either. Nya told me all about how she knew him from back in the day. That shit sounded funny as fuck. My bitch was always too beautiful for a nigga to not want to fuck and just be on some friend shit. But, right now my priority was getting back in power and making the niggas pay for not only putting me in a coma, but violating my wife, and killing Buck.

I was all the way fucked up being losing my nigga, my fucking brother. My anger towards him and the betrayal I felt didn't get any easier to deal with. I would forever be plagued with thinking that the one nigga I trusted had done some grimy shit that broke the fucking code behind my back.

The worst part was, he wasn't here to explain the shit to me. We could never get past it, well I never could, because Buck was dead. That shit hurt my heart still, despite the lies.

Nothing would ever be the same again. Nya was the only person I had in my corner right now, and shawty was proving what I already knew. That she was a thorough ass rider. The type of bitch that really holds shit down without complaint. Right now, I didn't have shit to offer her, but she was still here loving my ass.

I was never letting her ass go. When I said she was my wife, I meant that shit. A nigga like me never wanted a relationship, let alone a damn wife. But that's exactly what the fuck she was gonna be one day.

That's why I did some shit I never did with her earlier. I made love to NyAsia. Not just fucking, but that real heartfelt shit. Damn she had my ass wide open, I just hoped she continued to be here through thick and thin. Because this street shit wasn't going nowhere and me getting hit, falling off all that could happen at any time.

I was running late after finally getting some pussy, but Ron would have to deal with the shit. He had a headquarters where he did most of his business in Uptown. I had been here for sit downs in the past.

All three of us bosses switched up where we met every 3 months on a quarterly basis. That way we didn't have a choice but to trust the others somewhat, since we would each be vulnerable for a hit at the other's spot.

He had the place set up in a big ass old warehouse, disguised like it was just another legit business in the warehouse district. That way the shit didn't stand out more than any of the other businesses around. The front of the building was simple with a sign that read R.D and Son's Manufacturing.

The thing that made Ron weak to me was that he didn't build his shit from the bottom up like I had to do. This nigga got the shit handed to him from his pops. I understood how that shit worked and wasn't knocking him for it. Shit, if I had a son, I would probably do the same thing one day.

But there was still something different about a nigga who had to grind from nothing compared to one that put in work as a choice. The two didn't even fucking compare really.

It was around 5:00 in the afternoon, an hour after I was supposed to meet him. I knew that it wasn't the best way to start this shit out, but I had to get a taste of Nya's pussy earlier. It had been too damn long.

I texted Ron and got up with him about being late. He seemed fine with it. But we would see if he was on some fuck shit when I actually arrived.

All I had on me was my 38, but against a gang of niggas, odds weren't in my favor no matter how much heat I had. I went up to the front of the building and walked in like a regular ass customer would. When I stepped through the door, I saw Ron standing behind a counter talking to one of his workers.

The front of the building was set up like a legit manufacturing textile plant. Even when we walked to the back, he kept a few women in the main part running the machines.

"What's up?" Ron spoke up when he saw it was me that came in.

"Wahhh"

He came around the counter and stood in front of me giving me a sold ass handshake. He seemed straight so far, like this wasn't a setup.

He walked past me and gave a head nod indicating for me to follow him. I followed behind him and walked across the main open floor then through a door that led to the back office. Before we got to the office there was a game room with a pool table, living room set up, a wall to wall flat screen and a game system.

A couple of niggas playing a game of NBA2K, put the controllers down when they saw Ron walking through. They began to stand up and come to attention, but he waved them off.

"Nah, we cool. Shits good, right?!" he said the last part asking me, to make sure I wasn't on any bullshit either.

This shit said volumes about the nigga. He could have come at me on some superior shit, knowing that I was fucked up right now. But he was cool as hell, not trying to flaunt shit or act like he had more power than me. I respected that shit.

Now how he ran his shit was on him. I personally wouldn't have some niggas sitting around playing a damn game in the middle of the day when there was work to do. But that was on him, not me.

"We're good, nigga. Let me holla at you for a minute."

He walked through the room and I followed him into a large office. I closed the cherry wood door behind me. He really had this shit set up nice as hell. Inside his office was black leather furniture set and an oversized black desk. He sat down behind the desk and I sat in the chair across from him.

I started the moment I sat down. Time was the last fucking thing I had right now. All this shit needed to be handled as soon as possible so I could really focus my attention where it needed to be. On making more money and killing the bitch ass niggas that shot me.

"Smoke is my responsibility, so I won't ask you to handle that nigga. But, being as we been good and built The 3 C's together, I want to think in times like this we can look out for each other. Right now, I don't know how many niggas turned on me in my own crew. I'm asking you to provide me with some backup and information on what this nigga's been doing. I want this pussy nigga dead in the next 24 hours."

Ron sat back in his high backed office chair taking some time to think before he said anything in return. He folded his arms over his chest and shook his head. Our organization had been solid as fuck on both our ends the past 3 years so it made sense for him to back me on this shit.

"Yeah, I can do that. This partnership we got needs to get back on fucking track. That nigga already costing me and Marlo money. He's trying to lower prices and stepping on a lot of fucking toes, ya heard meh" He said referring to the other boss from Downtown.

Of the 3 of us, he was the hardest to figure out. I still didn't know if he was a real ass nigga or trustworthy. That nigga was off somehow, so I kept my distance for the most part and everything was only about business when I dealt with him.

"He's fucking with one of my niggas little sisters, she's only 16 bruh and he got her pregnant. Now my partna ready to go to war about the shit. Smoke's a fucking headache. So I'ma do more than just give you backup, I got you... I'll set up a meeting, making him think we're meeting about the prices and shit. Then during the meeting you get rid of his ass. He'll never see the shit coming if he don't know you're back." He finished.

This shit actually might work. Ron was offering more than I asked for, and I was gonna take him up on his offer. But I didn't for a second think that this wouldn't come with some kind of price. Nothing was for free. This meant later on I would owe him. I hated to owe a mothafucka anything, but I would keep up my end as long as he came through.

"He might think it's a set-up though, if he knows he got some beef going on over here with your people."

"Then we'll meet over at Calliope. There's a card game tonight, and he always in and out over there into some shit with another bitch he fucks with."

"You got eyes on him like that?" I asked, it seemed like he really was about to take his ass out anyway even without me.

"One thing I don't fucking play about is my bread, and that disrespect shit the nigga on. His days been numbered, mane."

I nodded my head. Smoke really was fucking up, and I bet his ass thought everything was good. He was dumb about shit that was obvious to others. He was too wild and reckless. Now, he was fucking with a juvie getting her pregnant, was some shit he should've never done. Especially with a nigga's sister that obviously was high up on this side of town.

I stood up and we shook hands, did our organizations solute and headed back out of the warehouse. Calliope was only a few minutes down the road from here. After hashing out details with Ron, he told me he would set the shit up for around midnight.

So in the meantime I would wait over near the spot and check out the surroundings on the low. I was a one man team tonight, even with Ron's backup. When shit popped off, I was the only shooter on this side now that Buck was gone.

-

I sat in my rental outside the corner store, and put in a call to Juan.

"Hola, What's up hermano?" He answered when the line picked up.

"Checking to see if you heard anything." I asked. He told me my "family" was gonna look into who was behind the attack on me and Nya.

"I just left from receiving a very interesting package. I'll be there in the morning. When I get in town send me your address and I'll share it with you."

"I'm ready for it, good looking, nigga." I said before hanging up.

Juan was my half-brother on my mother's side of the family. She was Puerto Rican and had moved to Louisiana to attend college. She came from a family that was involved in a lot of shit. Before she left for college, she had gotten pregnant and delivered a son at the age of 17. Her family raised the baby, while she came over here to get an education.

She never was cut out for that motherhood shit, from the beginning. To up and leave your baby with your family said a lot about what type of woman she was even if she was young.

She wasn't too young to fuck or to worry about going to school. She had the funds and support to take care of her kid but she chose not to.

Then she met my father her freshman year of college. I heard about all this shit from my aunt. She hated my mom's fucking guts. She saw her as the downfall for my father. Before her, he was the biggest hustler in the city. He ran the West Bank and was making moves to take over the rest of the city.

For whatever reason after I was born, my mama couldn't cope with the lifestyle and having a baby. She up and left my pops out the blue. After she was gone he got strung out on dope. Then started fucking with different crackheads.

That was how Jolie was born. Her mama wasn't shit either and left her. When I was 5 years old my father finally left me and Jolie with our grandfather after having different fiends watch over us for years. Shit was so fucked up.

I didn't have anything against my brother necessarily. I just didn't' feel any connection to the nigga. He always acted funny from the first time he got in contact with me. My mother's family was big time in the underground black-market worldwide.

They were royalty on the island. Juan's whole mannerisms and demeanor pissed me off. To me, respect and a bond had to be earned. The only family I really had was Jolie, Buck and Nya. The nigga was just an acquaintance, blood didn't mean shit to me.

I had to admit, Juan had really come through with taking care of shit when I as in a coma though. He didn't have to do none of the shit. We had a talk after I woke up while I was recovering. He wanted me to become more included in the family and get to know my grandparents, cousins all that shit. I told him I wasn't ready for all that, but would stay in contact with him more.

I wasn't turning my back on the idea altogether, but I didn't trust none of them yet. They knew about me from the jump and not one of them tried to help out or intervene in shit, even though they had the money to do so.

I'm glad the fuck they didn't now though. I wouldn't have had shit any other way than exactly how it turned out for me and Jolie. I was able to take care of my sister and if I wasn't there who knows what the fuck would have happened.

Thinking about Jolie, and having extra time on my hands made me feel like shit. This was the first time ever that I just let my sister do her own thing and be on her own.

Now that I had shit in motion to get things in order with my team and was getting information about who was responsible for the shit in Houston tomorrow, I needed my sister to come back in the fold.

Jolie was stubborn, but always softened up after talking about things. Her ass just loved to fucking talk. I pulled out my phone and hit her line next. Hopefully she would pick up so I wouldn't have to do the phone tag shit with her.

It was time that I boss the fuck up and get everything back moving right in all our lives. I was responsible for all the shit and I needed to start fucking acting like it.

Jolie

It was 2 months, 2 months since losing Buck and a month since realizing I was pregnant with his baby. After over a year of fucking and countless slip ups, the last time we had sex without a condom on Saint's birthday weekend, I ended up getting pregnant.

I remember that day like yesterday. How good my man looked and smelled. How mad I was after him making me cum back to back, because he busted inside me. Him coming up behind me and giving me that look of love and concern, the look of acceptance. We were just two people trying to cover up past wounds and old hurts, learning to love each other.

I laid on the big ass bed in the hotel room and cried freely. This was the same routine that had played out every day, every night since losing the love of my life. I still couldn't get past it even a little bit.

Every day I had panic attacks from remembering the bullets flying in the car and Buck pressing my head down, saving my life. Me watching him bleed to death and trying to get him to answer me, even though it was too late. This shit haunted my soul.

On top of losing him, I was alone, completely alone. I barely had anyone before but now my brother and Nya weren't even a part of my life. Neither one of them even knew I was pregnant. I couldn't bring myself to tell Nya because I was still furious with her. I still felt like she was partly to blame for Buck being taken away from me.

I knew deep down it wasn't her fault but it was easier to blame someone than nobody at all. She should have told me that the nigga behind all this knew her and was out to get her still. Then maybe Buck would have taken different precautions, who knows. Maybe it would have been the shit to save his life, but we would never know now.

My brother not speaking to me was killing me too. I even went as far as dialing his boy, Drew's number a few times trying to get in contact with him. Every time I called him, he at least answered. Drew was so kind and seemed to care, so over the course of the last few weeks the conversations got longer and we started talking about random everyday shit.

He was more than just the white boy from the hood that was cool as fuck, he was someone who was here for me. It wasn't on any sexual shit or anything like that, but it felt good to have at least one person that cared.

Our conversations had turned into daily events now and it was honestly the only part of the day I looked forward to. Each day, I woke up late, took a shower, changed, fixed my hair, ate and laid back down. I didn't go out of the hotel room, unless I had to.

It was really pathetic and sad as hell. By now, I had finally gone to the doctor. I had Drew take me, when he was in town the other day since he stayed out in Houston full time now. I didn't have a car or the motivation to go by myself. Just like I thought the moment I heard the heartbeat I was a mess, balling my eyes out on the table in the doctor's office and all.

I was almost 5 months pregnant and starting to show. The small bulge and extra thickness I picked up added to the meat I already had on my bones. Now I looked more like a certified BBW. I dint' even give a fuck how I looked either way.

Since Saint got shot, I had already filled out a FMLA for my job, so I didn't have to worry about that shit for at least a year. Who knew if I would ever go back?

Everything was so fucked up. I didn't know how I could bring a baby into the world, when I couldn't even get through a day. What good was I to the life growing inside me? I couldn't even take care of myself right now.

The thought of getting rid of the baby when I first found out crossed my mind, but there was no way I would kill the last part of

Buck I had left. I wanted marriage, stability all that shit for a child before I had one. But here I was all the way down and out having a baby.

My cell phone rang and when I grabbed it off the bedside table, I hesitated to answer. This is what I wanted, for Saint to talk to me. But I just hoped I was ready to face the shit and have this conversation for real. My brother was unpredictable and didn't hold back.

I took a deep breath, let it out and sat up against the headboard still wrapped in the covers.

"Hey"

"Damn, why you sound like that? I know your ass ain't in bed in the middle of the fucking day." He jumped right on my ass, calling me out.

"I was tired, but anyway... Let me start by saying I'm sorry... I..."

"Fuck all that, we're good. I love your ass too. I'm past it. You're my little sister that shit don't matter. It was still foul as hell, but it's done and over with. I can't be having you out there alone and shit. One more day, then I'm gonna send for you to head back this way."

"I've been good, Drew's been looking out and what do you mean?! You found who did this?" I asked getting excited.

82

My brother stopped me before I could even get going.

"One thing at a time, I'll be back home tomorrow. Then when you get here I'll fill you in on the other shit. You ain't gotta worry about a thing, I got you." He said reassuring me.

"Okay, when I get back I want to hear everything, and Saint, can you tell Nya I'm ready to talk?"

"Nah, shawty I ain't getting in ya'll shit. You tell her when you get here. Ain't nothing serious enough to fuck up our family, you heard meh." He told my ass with finality.

He was right, at the end of the day we were all we had out here.

"Love you." I finished with.

"Yeah yeah you too, big head"

I chuckled as I hit the end button to cut the call. Talking to my brother lightened my mood. I suddenly felt a surge of energy. I decided to get up and get the hotel room picked up. I only had about a week's worth of clothes on me, since getting in town from Puerto Rico. It was just some shit that Drew picked up for me. Saint was the one who sent him the first time to make sure I was good and set up here in Baton Rouge.

I couldn't wait to hear what information Saint got about who was behind everything. My brother never spoke over the phone about much, so I wasn't surprised that he wanted to wait. I was glad that he was getting shit back in order with his business too, there was nothing like being home.

I remade the bed and packed up my small duffle bag. Then sat back down on the side of the bed and rubbed my hand over my stomach. Maybe things could look up. Now that me and Saint were back on speaking terms I felt a weight lifted off of me. At least I had him again, the only thing left was for me to make shit right with Nya.

I hoped that I was able to put my feelings to the side and really reconcile with her. I still didn't know how the conversation was gonna go to be honest. Buck was still gone, the images forever in my mind, and I still felt like she might have been able to prevent it.

All there was to do now, was wait. I grabbed my phone again and called the familiar listening ear I had grown accustomed to. Maybe he was coming in town soon, and would be able to help break the news to my brother about being pregnant. Me and Saint might be on good terms now, but who knew how his feelings would change when I told him I was pregnant with his dead best friend's baby.

Nya

I stood up from being leaned over the toilet in the small ass bathroom. This was about the fourth time in the last month that I had been sick throwing up. I wasn't a damn genius, but I knew some shit was off. We had booked Terrell the room next to us, and I wanted to talk to him before I even talked to Saint about what I was thinking.

After Saint's shooting and my attack, when I flew back to New Orleans for Buck's funeral, I also went and filled out paperwork for Terrell to be homeschooled. Just for now. I didn't get into any details with the school, but at the time I had been raped, almost killed and Saint was on his deathbed. I couldn't send him to school every day, not knowing if his life was in danger. So I had to do what was in his best interest.

Terrell was being a trooper about everything and was doing the necessary homeschool work and the online courses I bought with it. He really was the fucking truth with his level of responsibility. He was a lot more mature than most 17 year olds. At least this was his junior year of high school and he would hopefully still have the opportunity to reenroll in school when all the dust settled behind this mess we were in.

I wiped my mouth with a tissue, opting not to trust the hand towel that hung on the rod. Who knew where that shit had been. I brushed my hand through my hair. My shit was back to being all natural just about 2 inches past my shoulders.

Jolie took the extensions out for me the night before we left for Puerto Rico. I had a lot of new growth with them in, but now my damn hair was really growing fast as hell and thicker than ever. That was just another sign.

I did the same sad ass deep breath that I did every time I thought about her. Jolie being mad and hating my ass, really broke my heart. Now I know how she felt, when he thought I turned my back on her for all those years.

I walked out of the bathroom and the hotel room altogether headed to Terrell's room next door. I went in the hallway and knocked a few times. Terrell came right to the door. It was around 6:00 and the usual time I had been coming to ask what he wanted to eat for dinner anyway. But this time when I came inside the room, I sat down and started talking about another subject.

"So... I got some news." I told him with my hand resting on my stomach. "You're about to be an uncle." I looked up at Terrell who was smiling big as hell.

"For real?" He asked still smiling. I nodded my head yes. "That's what the fuck I'm talking about!" He said, sounding genuinely happy and coming over to where I was.

I was relieved as hell that he was hyped about this shit, but his ass still needed to watch his mouth. I reached up and popped him on the arm for cursing.

"Damn... Dang." He joked rubbing on his arm like that shit really hurt. "I'm 'bout to be the best uncle. I hope you have boy, then I'ma teach him all kinds of shit. I mean stuff." He corrected himself.

I couldn't help smiling seeing how excited he was for me. For the longest it was just me and Terrell. He was like a son to me. I was worried that I wouldn't be able to pull off being a real mother. But now I didn't have a choice. Me and Saint never, not once used a condom. It never even came up. So it wasn't' a surprise that his ass got me knocked up so quick.

"I'm glad you're happy. And you know how we're still rocking. How do you think Saint's gonna take the news?"

Saint had been making it a point to take Terrell up under his wing, as a big brother without involving him in the street shit.

I loved the way that Saint took it upon himself to ask me about how Terrell was doing and check up on him in general. Even before the shooting he even started sparking up conversation with him whenever he came over to Jolie's. That was a real ass nigga for you. All that shit meant the world to me.

"You ain't told him yet?" He asked.

"No, I wanted to tell you first. Me and you have always been together through everything no matter what. This is gonna be your niece or nephew. I'm planning on telling him later when he gets back."

"I mean I don't know, does he like kids?"

"I don't even know, I mean I guess. He never shied away from responsibility before, but I don't know" I confided in him letting my uncertainty show.

"It'll be alright sis, that nigga loves you." He came over and gave me a light hug.

I stood up and said goodbye after telling him I ordered pizza for dinner. I had been craving some greasy ass pizza all day. The cravings had already kicked in. Yesterday I wanted some hot wings and pancakes but I didn't say nothing because I wasn't ready to tell Saint yet why I was wanting such weird shit.

Now I had to face this shit head on. I was never a coward about anything. It was better to get it out in the open, so I wouldn't be stressed about it. Saint was gonna do whatever he was gonna do regardless of what I said.

He had been gone most of the day. When the meeting ended, he sent me a text telling me he wouldn't be back until sometime in the morning. He didn't let me know nothing else, but I felt like there was some serious shit going on. It was like the two of us were connected even when were apart these days. I tried to keep my mind off where he was and what he was doing most of the day. But it kept wandering back to him anyway.

I ordered the pizza and laid back on the bed flipping through channels. I saw "Love and Hip Hop" was on but didn't keep it there long before turning to a wedding show. That shit wasn't even good anymore. Too many unknowns trying too hard to be the next Cardi B. Just like real life with so many frauds claiming they were this and that, but not really shit other than another hoe.

Saint

It was around midnight and I had been sitting watching the surrounding area for a couple hours already. Shit, I didn't have anything else to do anyway before I dealt with this nigga. Ron texted me a few minutes ago to let me know what building the card game was gonna be in.

I was familiar with Calliope, enough to find my way around. But not comfortable enough to be in and out all day drawing attention to myself. This wasn't my hood.

I wasn't trying to have a bunch of mothafuckas recognize me either. Now with it dark, I should be able to head over to where the card game was and not seem suspicious. As long as I played shit cool.

I needed to wait until after both Smoke and Ron got here with his niggas. That way he wouldn't get any kind of warning that flushed him out and fucked up my plans.

A few minutes later some cars I recognized pulled up on the curb across from where I was parked. I turned my head enough to watch the two whips and see who got out. I already had a pretty good idea, since one of them looked like Smoke's ride. He drove his flashy ass yellow Porsche. The shit was ugly as fuck if you asked me, but he always was about trying to show off how much money he was making.

Him and his little nigga started walking off towards the side of the building where the card game was supposed to take place. Around here it wasn't unusual for a card game to get hit for a robbery and shit. So it wouldn't seem like a set-up until it was too fucking late.

I waited about 30 more minutes before stepping out of the rental and walking over to the same place they entered. I was more than ready to get this shit over with and kill this nigga. Ron went to the spot right after Smoke and his nigga went in.

From watching the place, I estimated that there were probably around 15 more people inside the house. If some shit went wrong I was outnumber. But what the fuck was new.

I walked in blending in with the niggas standing around the table in the living room. All of the other furniture was cleared out besides the table and chairs for the niggas playing.

I scoped out my surrounding taking everything in. There were a few bitches posted up drinking and talking in the kitchen. Music was bumping, so when I slid in the already dark room, the niggas playing didn't even look up.

Smoke's back was turned to the door and now me. Just like Ron said, he looked out on this one. Him and his niggas were posted up on either side of the table. They were the only mothafuckas who looked my way, but still downplayed my appearance so others wouldn't notice yet.

Ron gave a slight nod, and that shit got Smoke's attention. He began to turn his head but before he could get the bitch all the way around my fucking pistol was pressed against the back of the bitch nigga's head.

I held the shit there.

"What the fuck is this shit about?" He sat looking straight ahead at Ron. He assumed this was set up by Ron since all he saw was a head nod, not who it was directed at. He still didn't know I was the one holding the tool.

One of Ron's goons stepped forward, but Ron held his arm up signaling him to stop and let Smoke be. I figured this was the nigga who wanted to get at Smoke for his baby sister and shit.

Ron shrugged and even though it was dark Smoke could see he was dismissing his question.

"Fuck you" He shouted, then tried reach to his back and stand up at the same time. I used my free hand and slammed his face against the table hard as fuck. Shit flew everywhere and all the niggas at the table stood up.

His nigga that he came with walked out of a back room with some bitch in front of him with his arms wrapped around her waist like they just got done fucking.

I still had Smoke's head pressed firmly down on the table as he squirmed to get free. He still didn't know it was me behind him. His homeboy recognized who I was and went to grab his heat. But as soon as he brought that shit out, the nigga standing next to Ron aimed his shit at his head and pulled the trigger.

His dome busted open and body fell to the floor. The bitch in front of him started screaming while other people ducked down to the ground to stay out of the way. It was only a matter of time before 12 got here now.

"Everybody out!" I shouted.

All the people hurried the fuck up and got on like I said, even Ron and his niggas started walking out.

"Nah, you're good, you can stay." I told the nigga who just took out Smoke's homeboy.

He stopped at the door and closed it. Unfortunately, now I only had a few minutes time to make this nigga pay for trying to play me pussy and overstep his damn position.

For trying to fucking play with a nigga like me.

I let off one in his arm that was on the table, then the other.

"AHHHHHHHHH! Damn Saint, I ain't ... Ahhhh fuck.... I was just holding... shit... down." He struggled to get out between the gasps of pain that were racking through his body.

"Snake ass nigga. I seen that pussy shit, disrespecting my bitch. Now you're out here claiming the whole fucking West Bank. Don't play scared now, bitch ass nigga. You're done. You know the rules."

I released his head and stepped back creating some space between his chair and my body. I wanted to look in his eyes when I saw the life leave them. I may have been a sick nigga, but I liked to watch a snake like him realize that they were dying. They would beg, plead and make a million fucking excuses. But it wasn't until they were really on the way out that they understood the consequences for the shit they did. It was time to make Smoke understand.

He stood up and turned around just like I wanted. I still had the gun trained on his head the whole time.

"Do that shit then." He tried to get bold all the sudden when he was begging a minute ago.

I waved the nigga on Ron's team over, "handle your shit."

He pulled out his heat and let off a round in Smoke's chest. He dropped to the floor after the second shot rang out, tearing through his chest. Falling to his knees, then doubling over onto his back.

I stepped over him and leaned down so I could see the shit closer. Then blasted the bitch in between the eyes. He died instantly.

""Preciate that fam." The nigga on Ron's team said.

"He deserved that shit, it ain't nothing, mane." I answered.

He slapped my hand and then both of us got the fuck on. Sirens weren't even heard yet. It shit was like hot and cold. When nothing was going on in the hood the police loved to stay up in it, harassing niggas for nothing. But when actual shit was going down, their asses couldn't be found. Oh well, it just meant more time for me to make my exit.

"Wake up shawty." I whispered in Nya's ear.

Then began sucking on her earlobe. I wanted to take off all her clothes and slide up in her wet pussy right now, especially after killing Smoke. There wasn't nothing like fucking after a kill.

But there was no way me or my bitch were about to be laid up in this bullshit ass motel another minute, when I already handled Smoke. Now we could go back home, where Nya belonged. She was just gonna have to move in with me.

I wasn't going back to only seeing my wife at the end of each day. I wanted her by my side every fucking minute possible. Terrell was welcome too, fuck it. Lil bro was cool as hell anyway.

I knew Nya had classes coming up this summer starting her first real college semester, and that was all the more reason why her ass needed to be around me on a more permanent basis. The problem was, I still had to head out to Houston for a while.

I didn't want her out there yet period. I still had to take care of the niggas after us and because she needed to settle in here first. College and shit was important. Her and Terrell needed to have some stability. When she brought it up to me, I was already thinking the same shit. I didn't give her an answer then but now that Smoke was out of the way, plans needed to be figured the fuck out.

I didn't know if I was gonna live out in Houston full time, for a few months or what.

Home was home and I still wanted to be in New Orleans more than anywhere else business might take my ass. There were too many uncertainties still with finding the niggas that needed to be dealt with out there.

"Mmmmmm, Saint, why you playing? You know my pussy's been waiting for you."

"Let me see." I reached down and slid my hand down her small ass pajama shorts and stuck a finger inside her. I started playing with her pussy moving in and out a few times, then rubbed my thumb against her clit as I slid it back out of her shorts.

Just that quick she went from being wet, to leaking ready to cum. Her body did whatever the fuck I wanted it to and responded to every touch from me. I love that shit. She was mine. I already knew no other nigga had her like I had her, she didn't even have to confirm that shit.

"I'ma take care of you when we get home."

I began picking up the small bags we had brought and looking around the room, making sure we weren't leaving anything behind. Nya was all the way awake and sitting up in bed by the time I was finished packing the shit.

"Home?" Nya asked rubbing her eyes and stretching, showing off her sexy stomach and part of the tattoo of my name above her pussy. Damn my bitch was bad. Just waking up she was a perfect ten.

"Everything's back on track, the nigga ain't a problem no more. We're going the fuck home. My home, your home. That shit is set in stone now. You done fucked up, getting with a nigga like me. You know I always get my way." I answered her.

I smiled big as hell at the annoyed expression she was giving me. She loved that shit though, Nya played like she couldn't stand me telling her what the fuck to do. But she wouldn't have the shit any other way.

"Since you're telling me all this, I got some news for your ass too..." She said with her funky ass attitude, twisting her neck with that ratchet shit. "You're 'bout to be a daddy."

I didn't have nothing to say to that shit at first. Damn, my shawty was pregnant with my seed, that was some real shit. I never strapped up with Nya. She was the only bitch I busted in after going raw, and now my baby was growing inside her.

My heart that I didn't even fucking let feel shit, swelled with pride. Fuck what you heard, this shit was some whole other feeling.

"You giving me my son? I wanna fuck the shit out of you now, come here."

She got up off the bed and strutted over to me. Nya only came right below my chin since I was so much taller than her. I

98

wrapped my arms around her waist and lifted her in the air. She locked her legs around my waist. I held her close kissing the shit out of her.

Her lips were soft as hell and tasted like the strawberry lip stuff she wore. Right now, if I died I would be perfectly content with the shit. This was the best moment of my life hands down.

I pulled back, "I love you girl."

"I love you too, daddy. Now give me the dick or I'm gonna take that mothafucka." She said serious as hell.

Nya

The doorbell kept fucking ringing. I was enjoying my damn sleep in this comfortable bed. After the night of sexing my man, I needed the damn rest. But whoever the hell was at the door was determined to wake my ass up. I finally rolled over and reluctantly opened my eyes.

"Damn, can't a bitch get some sleep." I grumbled to myself.

I threw my legs over the bed and stood up stretching my arms. According to the three at home pregnancy tests Saint made me take, I was officially pregnant. His ass was through the roof every time it came back positive like the nigga didn't already know.

The idea of being somebody's mother for real was growing on me the more encouragement Saint gave me. But actually carrying this baby was a different story. I didn't like being pregnant already and I still had a long damn way to go.

I was sick and tired as fuck all the time. It was so bad I was liable to fall asleep sitting on the damn couch in the middle of the day. So whoever was at the door better have a good ass reason for waking me up.

Things were already getting back to normal. But I didn't fool myself for a minute thinking that we were in the clear. The same

101

niggas that got at us before were still out there lurking.

I thought about that shit every day, trying to think of who was responsible. It made me think about a lot of shit that I buried away in my mind. I definitely made enemies out in Houston over all those years. I had to put in some work to keep me and Terrell safe. There was the time I handled a nigga that raped me all the way up to getting rid of Jaquan for that shit he pulled with Terrell.

I knew whoever it was wouldn't stop just because we were out in New Orleans. Me and Saint were both still breathing so they hadn't stopped shit. That was the crazy part, it was like they left me alive on purpose. I just hoped Saint got some answers before something else bad went down.

Saint met up with Juan the other day to get information. But he didn't tell me shit about the meeting when he got back. Instead, he switched the subject when I brought it up. He told me about how he saw Jolie afterwards.

All he was doing was trying to distract me. He didn't want me to know what he found out or who he found out was behind everything. Saint usually was an open book with me about any and everything. Now all the sudden, he didn't know shit about the one thing that was most important to me.

All of this was on me after all. No matter how many times he told me it wasn't my fault or tried to take the burden on himself. I wanted to be the one that made the niggas responsible pay just as much as he did.

He knew what the fuck he was doing with bringing Jolie up too. That was a sore ass subject for me. He caught me off guard with it and shut me the hell up quick. I didn't follow up with more questions about what Juan told him after that. But I planned on getting right back on his ass about the shit today when he got home. He wasn't slick.

As time passed I still held out hope that Jolie would forgive me. But the truth was, she might never get over Buck's death or find it in her heart to forgive me. She might always blame me for some shit I still didn't have a clue about who was responsible for.

But Saint told me, that Jolie wanted to talk to me. She was supposed to come over later today. We were finally gonna have a conversation. Who knew how it was gonna go. It might end up as bad as it did back in Puerto Rico.

The doorbell rang again, this time followed by banging. I know it wasn't the fucking police banging on our damn door because they wouldn't even bother with ringing the doorbell in the first place.

So whoever the fuck it was better have a good ass reason. It was only 8:00 in the morning. Saint left early to go out on the block and ride through the traps, trying to get shit back running right.

I grabbed the glock that Saint kept under his side of the bed. It was under the mattress loaded and ready to go. I was just as cautious and prepared as he was.

I made my way downstairs still wearing only the sheer, black and lace negligee.

"Who is it?" I called out.

Nobody answered, so I looked through the peephole.

Standing on the other side of the door was some Spanish looking bitch. She was taller than me, and skinny as fuck like one of those bone thin models. She was pretty in the face but nothing special. She looked like an uppity boujie bitch.

I didn't know for sure, but I had a pretty good idea why she was here and I bet anything it had something to do with my man's dick. So far, I hadn't had to deal with the hoes and hoodrats that were after Saint. He made it seem like I was the only woman he wanted and I was pretty confident that he hadn't cheated on me. But I wasn't a fool. I knew there were some skeletons in his closet, just like there was in mine.

I held the gun behind my back and opened the door. Standing in the doorway, letting the bitch get a good ass look at me and see what the fuck my nigga really liked. It most definitely wasn't her little boy, looking ass. She didn't have any ass or body on her.

She wasn't the type of woman that I had ever seen Saint fucking with in the past when we were younger. But I also knew these niggas didn't discriminate, pussy was pussy.

"What are you doing here? I thought this was Saint's house." She said acting all entitled and shit. She had no fucking clue who I was.

"Bitch, this is OUR home. Why the fuck are you on MY doorstep is the real question! Waking me up early as hell, asking me shit. What the fuck's wrong with you?!" I spoke up getting louder.

"I'm not answering your questions. Where is Saint, LA PERRA?" She chose to ignore me.

I could barely understand the ugly hoe with her thick Spanish accent but I knew that last shit was disrespectful. She really fucked up with that fucking attitude.

I pulled the glock out from behind my back and pointed it straight at the bitch's head. She took a small step back and held up her hands in surrender. Fear written all over her face.

Before she took her second step backwards, I reached out with my free hand and grabbed the back of her head, snatching up a wad of her long brown hair. I didn't give a fuck if she knew Saint had a bitch or not. She was never gonna speak on my nigga again or come at me disrespectful. She should've never talked shit to someone like me if she wasn't ready to fight. I was all the way about the shit.

I held the gun to her forehead, "Don't ever ask about MY NIGGA AGAIN! I will kill your ass next time. Forget you ever met him." I warned.

Then I let go of her hair pushing her back in the process. She wasn't about shit and wasn't even worth the fight. She better get the fucking message, because I wasn't the one to play about the shit I said.

I would take her ass out in a heartbeat if she tried to come between me and Saint. I waited half my life to find the love I finally had with him. The peace he brought in my life and relationship we had was everything to me. No hoe was coming between that.

She held back the tears in her eyes, fixed her hair the best she could, then looked back up in my direction. I had to give it to the bitch, she tried to get it together and get rid of the fear that was showing just a moment ago. All of the sudden trying to act like I didn't scare the fuck out of her.

She gave my body another look, this time betraying her jealousy. My body was on point and since being with Saint he had built up my self-image more than ever before. I was beginning to see what everyone else saw and that was a beautiful woman.

"He'll have to see me now that I'm carrying his child." She said looking me right in the eyes with s smirk and resting her hand on her stomach.

Oh fuck no. No way was this Spanish bitch pregnant by my nigga and if she was, she wouldn't be for long.

I dropped the gun and took off after her. She tried to run, but I was too quick and got ahold of her within a few steps. I started swinging back to back, throwing punches to her face. It was like I blacked out swinging, landing punch after punch. She fell to the ground.

"Talk shit now hoe!"

She didn't even land one single punch or try. Instead she held her hands over her face. I finally stopped after she wasn't moving anymore and leaned down spitting on her body while I stood over her, breathing hard from the ass whooping I just put on Saint's side bitch.

Fuck him and the bitch. He had me out here fighting some hoe in the front yard. This nigga really needed to control his hoes. I wasn't going for the disrespect or the cheating for that matter. I should never have to be confronted with some shit like this.

I straightened my hair and fixed my clothes back, similar to how the bitch did before I jumped on her and started giving her the business. She should have known better to come with that bullshit to a hood bitch like me.

I turned around about to go back inside, and then remembered the girl said she was pregnant. I went back to where she was laid out on the walkway in front of the porch.

Then brought my leg back and landed one kick straight to her stomach as hard as I could. She immediately dropped her hands to her stomach trying to shield the shit. But it was too late.

"AHHHHHHHHHHH, AHHHHHHHH, NOOOOOO." She cried out, screaming a gut wrenching scream.

I didn't waste another minute standing in the hoe's presence. Instead I walked back inside and closed the front door behind me. I left the gun lying on the floor in the foyer and went upstairs to grab my phone. I hit send and called Saint's ass.

"Come get your baby mama..." Click.

Saint

What the fuck was Nya talking about? She ended the call just as quick as it began talking about my "baby mama". Damn, now I needed to get the fuck home and see what bullshit she was on. I really had no clue, but her ass had been more emotional since finding out she was pregnant.

This morning wasn't going smooth already. Riding all over town trying to round up loyal niggas that I could trust enough to put back to work or bring in new was hard enough. Not having my day one nigga by my side wasn't helping. Buck would have been making moves right alongside me. At least Drew came out for a couple days to help weed out any week links.

"Yo, I gotta head home for a minute. You got this? I'll be back around 3 to make sure shit's a go."

I looked over at Drew who was counting all the dough we just picked up from the traps. We brought that shit to the downtown house.

I was able to bring back the few niggas that Smoke tried to put out of my fucking team for staying loyal to me and not following behind his bitch ass. He fucked up keeping them alive, but his ass wasn't built to be a boss. He didn't understand what moves needed to be made and that was why he should have never tried to take what wasn't meant for him. Niggas like him could never be successful at the top, they didn't have the mind or heart for it.

"Damn, the wife got you sprung like that? Drew started laughing his ass off.

"Fuck you, I'ma be that sprung nigga getting loyal pussy every day, ain't nothing like a bitch who will hold you down for life. Take it from me. Nya's pregnant too. So it's really whatever my bitch wants now, ya heard meh." I said giving a head nod.

Shit, getting a taste of pussy and fucking did sound good as hell right now. But Nya wasn't like herself on the phone so I had a feeling I was coming into bullshit on this one.

"You're right about that, and congratulations man." Drew said standing up slapping hands with me. "I can't wait until I find a real ass bitch to hold me down. First thing I'm doing is getting her ass pregnant." He was serious as hell.

His phone started ringing and he hit the ignore button. It started ringing again right away. Back to back.

I raised my eyebrows, "See what the fuck I mean." I returned the laugh.

"Nah, lil' baby ain't my girl, just a friend and she ain't like none of these other hoes."

He must really be feeling old girl. Drew had plenty of bitches after him. He had game for a white boy, but he didn't let any of them around his business shit and I respected the way he handled himself. A man that moved sloppy in his personal life usually was just as reckless with his work.

"Answer your shit, you're 'bout done and I'm out. Drop the bread off to the club and we'll meet up at the restaurant before catching the flight. Be on the lookout for how shit gets moving."

I turned and headed out of the house, closing the door behind me and looking around at my surroundings. Ever since getting shot the fuck up, I had was even more cautious. If I was paranoid before, now I was fucking crazy.

On the drive home I kept thinking more about the moves I needed to make in the next few days out in Houston. It was gonna be a lot of unknowns and I needed to be ready to settle this shit once and for all.

Before I knew it, I was already pulling up into my driveway.

Fuck!

Martina was laid out in my mothafuckin' front yard.

I hopped out of the jeep and walked over to where she was laying. She was awake, eyes open looking pitiful as hell. It had been about 30 minutes since Nya called me, so she was probably out here for that long.

Martina's face was all fucked up and swollen. She had dark black and blue circles around her eyes and dried blood crusted up on her cheek. Her hair was all over the damn place. It looked like she got her ass whooped, but nothing that should cause her to be laid the fuck out for this long, especially since she was wide awake now.

I knew Nya did this shit to Martina. She was a beast for real. Martina should've never showed up at my fucking house. I didn't even invite her over when we were fucking. She shouldn't know where the fuck I lived to begin with and must have used her pull in the cartel to find my spot. It wasn't even listed in my government or street name, it was in Jolie's.

Martina deserved what the fuck she got for trying to pop up here. She was foul as hell and out of her damn mind.

She looked up at me and reached her arm up, like she was waiting for me to help her ass up. This bitch was fully capable of getting up, she wasn't that fucked up. Since we were in my hood nobody got in my business like that and called an ambulance.

113

The last thing I wanted was some heat my way over this girl. She was like a thorn in my fucking side.

"Get the fuck up Martina, and get out of my yard. You should've never brought your ass here in the first place."

"Why are you doing this to me?" She said through tears, standing to get up.

Finally realizing I wasn't here to help her and hopefully understanding that I didn't give a fuck about her.

I was here because my fucking wife called, not anything to do with her ass. I already told her shit with us was a wrap. I stopped fucking with her months ago and never thought twice about it.

I wasn't even dealing with her pops no more and had another connect altogether. Martina really should have got the message by now. I was nice before when I let her down easy, but now she was doing dumb shit like showing up at my fucking house.

"Like I said get the fuck on, and don't bring your ass back. I don't want shit to do with you shawty." I turned to walk away.

Martina reached out, touching my shoulder, trying to push up on me right out here. She slid her hand down to the bulge in my pants and tried to grab my dick. I stopped walking and tilted my head to the side. This bitch was fucking crazy, damn.

Before I stopped her from making a fool of herself further, the front door opened and Nya came out on the porch. Looking fucking beautiful, like a queen aiming my Glock in our direction.

I couldn't even tell if the shit was pointed at me or Martina. She had a look in her eyes that I had only seen one time before, and that was before she killed that fuck nigga back in Houston.

Nya walked over to where we were, stopping a few feet in front of me. She was wearing her black little ass shit that she slept in. It was fucking see through, all out in the open for the damn neighbors to see what was meant for my eyes only. I was ready to scoop her ass up and take her the fuck back inside.

She held the gun in Martina's direction, then looked me in the eyes with a look of sadness. Nya covered that shit right back up with the look of steel she had before. Showing no weakness, nothing but the look of a shooter.

"I told you about this shit and now MY nigga told you to get the fuck on. So do that shit!"

Nya moved her aim down and pulled the trigger hitting Martina in the lower leg. Martina jumped back and screamed out in pain,

"What the fuck, you shot me, ahhhhhhhhhhhhhh!!!" She looked up surprised and in pain from what Nya did.

"Get the fuck in your car. Don't forget next time it's a head shot." She said ice cold.

Martina looked at me then ran to her car the best she could, leaking and half skipping to it. She probably couldn't fucking drive, but Nya kept the tool aimed at her car to motivate her to figure the shit out real quick. All the way until she managed to pull around the corner, speeding off fast as fuck.

When her car was out of view, Nya finally lowered the gun. I reached out and grabbed her arm then the gun and took that shit, tucking in in my waistband.

Nya was almost unresponsive to me. She didn't show not a single ounce of emotion. This shit was fucking with her bad. Not having to shoot the girl, it was something deeper than that. I had seen her kill a nigga with her bare hands without the look she had on her face now. It was like I was watching her mentally put up the walls again that she just took down.

"Nah, shawty you ain't out here like that. I released my grip on her arm and instead held her hand ready to lead her inside the house. She still didn't say shit but I saw a tear fall from her eyes. She let if fall.

"Let's go inside."

She yanked her hand away and walked ahead of me back into the house mad as hell.

When we got in the house, we both went into the living room and sat down across from each other in a damn stare off. She was sending evil ass looks my way and I stared right back trying to figure out what the fuck I could say that wouldn't piss her off or push her away more.

Nya wasn't weak or open to love and shit besides with me, my sister and Terrell. We were her family. I knew how she felt. I always knew how she felt. She was scared that I was gonna hurt her worse than any other shit she had ever been through.

I knew this shit, because that was the exact same way she had my ass. We were vulnerable to more pain than we ever wanted to feel.

"I mean I know you're a nigga and loyalty don't mean shit to you, but damn. You're out fucking raw and shit, not even giving a fuck about what you got at home. Trying to have a bunch of fucking baby mamas. I ain't with that shit Saint."

"It ain't even like that..." I started, but she straight up got up and walked the fuck away.

Nya didn't want to hear shit I had to say. It didn't matter that I didn't cheat on her with Martina. She was right I was a nigga and

I did fuck up that one time in Houston that she still didn't know about. But that shit was done.

After I got shot and the girl I was messing with died that night in the hotel room, I vowed to myself not to disrespect Nya again. Even by getting my dick sucked. As bad as this shit today looked I was innocent on this one. She didn't want to hear shit I had to say right now though.

I don't know what the fuck gave her the idea that Martina was pregnant. But I never fucked raw and busted in a bitch besides her.

I followed behind Nya and found her in the kitchen standing against the counter biting her bottom lip. She had her arms folded, in deep thought. I came up on the other side of the counter and looked at her again.

"I'm telling you I ain't cheating on you. I never fucked her. You're all I want, I put that shit on everything. That bitch was someone I fucked before. She's my old plug's daughter, I ended it before me and you." I pointed between me and her.

"So she wasn't pregnant?"

"No fucking way, I never busted in the bitch, on God."

"Since we've been together you said you ain't fucked her... Have you messed with anyone else? And tell me the fucking truth,

118

keep shit all the way real. I mean I ain't fucked with no nigga, I'll let you know that right now." She stated in a challenge.

I brushed my hand over my hair, out of habit and looked down. I wasn't gonna lie to her. I couldn't sit here, look her in the eyes and do that shit. I respected her too fucking much. I wasn't fucking with any hoes now though.

I looked back up, "Some bitch gave me head, before I got shot in Houston, but nothing went further. I ended that shit. I don't give a fuck about anybody but you shawty, you heard meh. You're my fucking wife."

She nodded her head a few times continuing to look at me. "Okay, okay." She came around to where I was and gave me a kiss on the cheek. "I love you, but right now I just need to focus on school, Terrell and the baby. I need some time to think about shit."

Was she really serious? Think about shit. For what. There was no getting out of this. She was with me for life. I slammed my fists into the counter, causing the dishes on it to slam and crash onto the floor breaking into pieces. That shit startled her and she backed up.

I was pissed. When she fucked up on my birthday I didn't try and walk away, I got over the shit. Because that was what the fuck we had. We were in this shit through thick and thin, wasn't no walking away. Nya's sometimey ass needed to get her shit together.

She could be mad, sleep in another bedroom, give me the silent treatment, whatever the fuck she needed to get past me hurting her with what I did in Houston. Here she was pregnant with my seed talking about needing time. She wasn't getting no fucking time apart.

I looked at her, "You ain't getting no fucking time baby, this shit is for life. This love we got. Remember what the fuck I said?! Ain't no going back now. So you want to be mad, be mad, but then get over the shit."

"You don't fucking get it Saint, I love you. I love you too much, more than myself even. I can't deal with the shit that comes with you. I'm not like those other bitches. I will go to jail behind you. I will kill every fucking hoe that you even look at. I got a baby to think about now. I can't do this shit for no nigga. I can't."

She started crying more. I walked over to her and held her for a few minutes, letting her words sink in while I comforted her.

Then I let go and walked out of the house. I had to walk away. Not for good, but for now. Nya wasn't in this shit, so how the fuck could I be. She told me how she really felt. She didn't want to do this shit with me or to forgive me for one slip up before we got serious. Yeah it hurt like hell. But I couldn't let a bitch bring me down, not even the one who held my heart.

Jolie

I was on my way over to my brother's house, to meet up with Nya. It was time to put this shit behind me. I had already told her how I felt about the shit back in the hospital even before my brother's recovery and I still felt the exact same way. I wasn't holding onto as much animosity towards her anymore. But I didn't know if we would be cool after this afternoon. I hoped shit could get back to normal, but I was still hurting behind Buck's death.

I knocked on the door and waited a good minute before ringing the doorbell. Nya came to the door, wearing some kind of nightgown and robe. It was already late afternoon, so for her to be still wearing bed clothes let me know some shit was off.

She had her hair down, rocking her natural shit. She still looked beautiful without a doubt, but her demeanor was just sad. I knew this, because it was the same way I had looked and felt for the last few months.

"Hey."

"What's up girl?"

"Come on in. I'm glad you're here." Nya said, sounding sincere.

I followed her into the house and sat down in the living room on the opposite side

122

of where she sat. She folded her legs under her on the oversized chair and leaned back ready to talk from the jump. I was here for that, so I might as well dive right in.

I tucked my hair behind my ears since today I wore it down and out. I stayed posted up on the edge of the couch, not quite comfortable yet. I wanted her to know where I stood.

"I want you to know, I still love you. But to keep shit real, I still feel the same way about how shit went down. Buck ain't here and a part of me blames you for that. I'll always wonder about the what ifs... I want to get over it. But how can I?!"

I left an opening. I wanted her to tell me how to forgive her and let this shit go. It was killing me hating my best friend again, like I did for all those years when I thought she betrayed me. This time it was worse though, because she might have fucked up the best thing in my life.

"If there was anything I could have done to save Buck I would be the first person to do that shit, don't you think? He was family to me. I don't know who the fuck did this shit. I've been blaming myself too. But you know what? The truth is, the niggas that shot Saint, that raped me, they're the mothafuckas responsible, NOT ME!" She pointed at herself. Nya always used her hands to talk when she was really into the shit she was saying.

"Buck was a real ass nigga, handling shit the best he could at the time. He knew that all of us were still targets. Him and Drew were doing everything they could to find them. I didn't know who was behind it and I still don't. Shit, I'm sorry he's gone, but this ain't on me. I was blaming myself, but Saint helped me realize that shit like can always happen in this lifestyle. This could be any of our last days." She looked as frustrated as she sounded.

She was absolutely right. Everything she said made sense, but I still couldn't let go yet. I wanted to, but it was easier to be mad than really let the pain swallow me completely.

I stared off in the other direction away from her, thinking in silence. I let tears fall like they always did and absently rubbed my stomach thinking about our baby. The baby Buck would never get to meet or hold. I was heartbroken, but hopefully with time I could heal. With the life growing inside me, maybe I could find a way to move forward.

"So you're pregnant." Nya interrupted my thoughts.

"Huh??, uhhh, yeah. I am. Look, Nya I don't know if I can let go, but I'm willing to try. Right now I'm not there, and I don't know if I'll ever be the same person I was. But I want to be. That's all I can give you right now. We're good. We'll see how shit plays out." I answered, being as honest as I could be.

"Thank you... And Jolie, you're 'bout to be an aunt too." She said with a smile rubbing her own stomach. I returned her smile.

Hearing her say she was pregnant right along with me, helped to switch up my train of thought. I always wanted us to have babies that grew up close. We talked about that shit when we were still teenagers, and now it was actually happening.

"Damn, what did my brother say to that?" I wanted to know.

Her face changed and the sadness I noticed when she first opened the door returned. She tried to cover it up, just like she always did. Trying to put on a strong front.

"That nigga's already trying to boss my ass around even more. It's gonna be a hard ass 8 months. He's talking about having his son. Like how the hell does he know he's gonna get a son? Just 'cus he said so! I swear he's so damn hard headed."

She was holding some shit back. I could tell, by not saying anything else.

"Girl don't I know it. I'm worried about how he's gonna act when I tell him about me having a baby by Buck. He's just now getting over us keeping it a secret. So I'm gonna tell him today, fuck all that secret shit. I learned my lesson. But I hope he can accept this."

"He will. You know how Saint is. Above everything else, that nigga is gonna take care of us." She said half-jokingly with a chuckle.

Yeah some shit was definitely off. But I was gonna let it be. It wasn't none of my business and right now me and Nya were just back on speaking terms. I wasn't gonna pry.

After another hour of conversation and making plans to go shopping to buy some baby stuff, I ended up leaving a whole hell of a lot better than I came. Feeling another weight lifted up off me. We even hugged at the door before I left. It was refreshing and just what I needed, to talk to my best friend. I missed her, even while hating her ass.

She did give me some more hope that things would get better. She reminded me that Saint was looking for the niggas responsible, even as we spoke. She told me that she heard him talking to Juan about a lead he had. But she wasn't sure. Saint was trying to keep her in the dark with this shit and she wasn't happy about it.

I hopped back in my car and drove the few streets back to my house. It felt good to

126

be home, but lonely as hell. Terrell even up and moved out, and was staying over with Saint and Nya now.

I didn't' blame him, he wanted to stay with his sister. He really wouldn't go nowhere but where Nya was. Their bond was a lot like mine and Saint's. Where she was his keeper and Saint was mine.

Drew's name popped up on my phone screen, as it vibrated on the center console. I answered in a good ass mood.

"You good now?" He asked.

Earlier, I had called Drew to talk about me facing shit and meeting up with Nya. Of course he was there to listen and keep shit real with me. That was the shit I appreciated the most about our friendship. He was always a hundred percent with me, no sugar coating shit he thought I would want to hear.

"Yeah, thanks for checking on me."

"You know you can count on me..." He paused. "I'm heading back out to Houston for a minute, so I won't be around."

"What time are you leaving? Your ass better call me when you touch down." I told his ass.

He always waited to call me way afterwards and I liked to know his flight landed. Flying made me nervous as hell and I didn't even like catching a flight unless I had to. I would much rather drive if I could. Going on vacation once a year was about all the damn flying I did. It was scary as hell to me, not to be in control.

"Yeah, I'll get up with you, but look... I think we gotta cool off talking for a while."

"What? Why? I mean, I know I got a lot of shit with me, but I really enjoy our conversations and your friendship means a lot to me."

I was totally caught off guard. He had told me from the jump that he was gonna be here for me, for anything and I really started depending on his level headed talks. Now he was trying to pull away. Maybe I was interfering with him and his bitch or something.

"If it's a problem with you and your girl, I'll talk to her and let her know we're just friends."

I heard him take a deep breath into the phone, sounding frustrated.

"Nah, it ain't like that. Me and Ashley are a wrap. I'm feeling you... beyond the friends shit. I know shit's fucked up, you getting over my man's death and I'm working for your brother. I don't expect shit from you. It's just better if I keep my distance, so you can get your head together. I'm still here for you. But I'm not trying to get in too deep, you feel me?

I was speechless. I had no idea Drew had feelings for me. I never even got that vibe from him. Maybe I just wasn't looking for it.

I had never been with a white man before. Drew wasn't the typical white boy. He was all man and to anyone else sexy as hell with his street edge and good looks. He was a real ass gangsta all the way around.

I just never looked at him like that. Now that he was telling me this shit, I didn't know how to feel. I wasn't ready to go there with any man. I was still grieving the love of my life and pregnant with a baby to think about. I didn't have any room to hear the shit he was telling me.

I sat there on the other line, quiet not answering or responding. Drew was right. It was better if he fell back and we kept things on a friend's only basis.

"You ain't never held shit back before, say what's on your mind girl."

As I turned into the road that led to my house, I finally answered him.

"You're right. It's better if we cut out our talks and you fall back... But Drew... I do care about you. But you're right... not in that way. I never thought about being with anyone but Buck. And now I don't know if I'll ever be in a relationship with another man. It's nothing personal to you."

"Jolie you're good. You ain't gotta explain shit to me. I'll see you around. And if you need me, call. You know I got you."

We ended the call and after hitting the end button, my happy mood instantly deflated. I felt like I lost a friend with that conversation. It was like taking a step forward and one back today.

Drew had been my rock over the past couple months. I knew I was going to miss him. But it wasn't fair to him to expect him to be here for me with how he felt and me not return that shit back. I had been on the other end of not receiving the affection back when me and Buck first started messing around.

Drew was tall with an olive complexion and athletic build that suited him. From the time I first saw him a few years ago, he always pulled the most ratchet bitches. I mean nothing but straight hood bitches. We weren't close back then, but even now his bitch Ashley stayed bringing drama his way. He definitely loved him a black woman, but I just couldn't be the good woman he needed in his life.

I got out of the car and made my way inside. My mood was fucked up now, but at least it was another day I made it without buck. So it was a win no matter what.

I sat my purse down on the table in the kitchen and walked my ass upstairs nice and slow. The cleaning and laundry would have to wait until tomorrow because this baby was taking all my energy today. I laid down sprawled out on my king-size bed and called the Chinese restaurant down the road that delivered out here.

I ordered some Chicken wings and friend rice with loe mein. I was craving Chinses food like every other day with the baby. It was crazy since I never even really liked Chinses food, but Buck's ass loved the shit.

I sat down and kicked back my feet enjoying the solitude. This was my life. Alone, and learning to be content with the shit. My mind wondered back to what Drew said to me.

He dropped that bomb on me and a small part of me was intrigued by what he said. It did feel good to have a man want me at my worst. He saw me when I looked a mess and was pitiful. I was definitely gonna miss him in my life, but I guess it was for the best.

Tonya

There had been no real trace of Saint or that bitch he was fucking with in months. But the other day that shit changed. I overheard Julius on the phone mention his name.

We just finished fucking and I pretended to be asleep when I heard his phone vibrate. He got up off the bed and I listened to every word he said. Of course Julius's over cautious ass cut that shit short by putting on his pants and walking out of the room almost right away. But not before I caught the name "Saint" as he stepped out.

Julius was into some serious shit here in Houston. I was still figuring out how big he was. He was private as hell and didn't give up information easy. I knew for a fact I wasn't his main bitch or probably even his side chick. I was just something to do, but I was okay with that. He provided me with a few hundred here and there every week and that was enough for now.

All I was looking for from him was help with Saint and his hoe. The thing that got me the most about his bitch was that she walked around like she was better than me. Even the few times I saw her around other bitches, it was the same shit.

She had this confidence and arrogance, like she didn't come up out of the hood just like my ass. Yeah, I could tell she was a hood bitch too. But she acted like she was better. I couldn't stand them boujie hoes that looked down on bitches like me who had to do what the fuck we had to do to get a bag. Now she had Saint following behind her ass like she was perfect.

Ever since I heard Julius say Saint's name I had been trying my best to stay as close to the nigga as possible. That way when some shit came up involving him, Julius had no choice but to tell me about the it.

I brought up Saint's name out of the blue yesterday, randomly asking if he had heard anything. Julius slapped me in the damn face for being "a nosey bitch", calling me out of my name. What the fuck did he expect though? We started fucking around because we had a common enemy. Now he wanted to switch up and flip the script. Fuck that.

So this morning, I decided to go over to Saint's condo and keep a lookout for any sign of him. My sister left a lot of fucking information in her diary. She was dumb as hell for keeping shit like this. When I died my secrets were gonna be buried with my ass.

In it she wrote down the address for his place, probably from when Saint first gave it to her. They weren't fucking around heavy, but the nigga at least gave her his shit.

He was fucking her raw. I wonder how his bitch Nya would feel about him having another woman pregnant. Even if the shit was terminated early with her being gone, it might still cause a reaction in the hoe.

It just happened to be my luck that I saw the white boy that Saint kept around him coming out of the building Saint lived in. That definitely piqued my interest. So I waited longer and sure enough, within a few minutes my fine ass nigga was walking out.

My pussy and mouth salivated looking at him. I was ready to hop out my car and make my presence known. But instead I stayed put and chose to watch Saint's moves a little longer before exposing myself. I needed his bitch to show her face before I came out of the woodwork.

My cell began ringing with the tone I set for Julius.

"Hey bae".

"Where the fuck you at?" He asked sounding like the cold ass nigga he was.

Julius might've thought he put fear in my heart, but I wasn't the bitch for that shit. All that putting his hands on me wasn't nothing new. I had been through all of that when I was coming up. So he needed to calm the barking he was doing down. But I played my position well and made him think I was the obedient bitch he expected.

"I'm on my way home. Why? Is something wrong?" I cooed trying to calm his temper.

"Bitch stop lying, I got eyes on you now. What's really good?" He surprised me.

I looked from side to side, with the phone still to my ear trying to see if he was telling the truth. I didn't see a damn thing out of ordinary or one of his cars anywhere in sight. I took a deep breath and began to respond, "What are..."

A tapping on the window startled the fuck out of me and when I looked to the side again, this time the mothafucka was staring down at me. What the hell was going on? This nigga really was on his shit.

I rolled down the window and ended the call. Keeping quiet, I waited for him to say something first. Julius took his time staring my ass down with an evil ass look on his face.

"Get the fuck back to my crib now" He kept his voice low and even but it damn sure was menacing. I hesitated and thought about going against his demand. But now wasn't the time. I wasn't trying to get my ass beat to a pulp.

He must have seen my hesitation though and just that quick he lifted his right hand and pointed his pistol in my face while he stood all the way up, causing his face to go out of view. The barrel was inches from my mouth.

My body shook and I put my hands on the steering wheel trying to play the shit off. Julius leaned back down again still keeping the gun trained on me to look me in the eyes making sure I got the damn message. All I could do was nod my head and agree.

One thing I didn't fucking like was having a gun pointed at me. I loved my life way to fucking much for that shit. I could put up with a lot of shit, but I didn't want to die. Especially not behind a nigga or bitch. I might be a scary bitch, but I was a living one.

Julius lowered his hand and put that shit back in his jacket pocket. But the nigga kept his hand on it still. He stepped back a few feet and stood still waiting for me to pull off. I raised my window and put my fucking foot to the pedal.

This nigga had my heart beating fast as fuck. After pulling away and heading around the block, I finally got control of that shit. My mind was racing.

Julius was really trying to control my moves and keep me out of his way with this Saint shit. That meant that there was more to the shit between them that I didn't know about. Why was he after Saint? It had to be something serious. But I didn't want Saint to die.

I made the decision just that quick, to go against his order and head over to his place. Instead I turned in the direction back to my aunt's house, with one thing on my mind. Nya needed to go now! This was probably the best chance I would get to handle her ass.

I didn't spot her with Saint, but I had a good ass feeling she was here in Houston staying right up under him. Shit, she probably was laid up in his spot right now, or at least I was betting on that shit. It was all I had to go on.

I had to hurry the fuck up and get up with my aunt Renae before I went off the grid in hiding for a minute. She was the only person who could help me now. I couldn't let her know the details because it would put her at odds with Julius and her boyfriend. I just hoped she was on board to help me, despite that shit. I still was gonna come out on top of this shit, getting every fucking thing I wanted.

Fuck niggas.

Nya

Today me and Jolie went shopping and finally were able to catch up on more of what we had missed over the last few months being at odds. It felt great to have my best friend back in my corner even if shit was still awkward at times.

We loved each other and so that was all that mattered, time would heal some of the hurt, I was sure of that shit. I knew first-hand how time could heal the heart from what I went through in the past.

I looked out the window staring at nothing in particular. It was a cloudy, gloomy ass day that matched my mood. The heat here was making it miserable to be outside. I couldn't imagine what it would be like if I was further along in my pregnancy like Jolie. She wore it well though and her mood seemed to improve with every passing day.

It was like with one thing going right the other was off balance in my life. Right now me and Saint weren't speaking at all. I hadn't heard from his ass for the past 3 days. Not since our argument and he left the house. I hadn't even had an opportunity to make shit right.

My pride wouldn't allow me to call him either, even if a part of me knew I was wrong for the shit I said. But it was how I felt at the time and still felt.

Instead I focused on making sure Terrell was getting back settled in school alright and planning out my summer courses. I only had a few weeks before they officially began.

Since getting back from the mall earlier and finally opening up to Jolie about what was going on with me and her brother, Saint had been on my mind nonstop. There was no distractions that made me stop wondering about him now. It didn't help that she told me how fucked up he was behind the shit I did too.

It turned out after she left from meeting up with me the same day me and Saint had the big ass fall out she followed through with breaking the news of her pregnancy to him. She bit the bullet and got up with him right away that same night. She ended up calling him and they met up for dinner together before he flew out to Houston.

I knew his ass was going to Houston, but I didn't for once think shit would be all the way bad between us so fast. In the blink of an eye we went from being perfect to not even fucking talking.

This shit hurt me to the core, but the thought of how much I loved him scared the fuck out of me. I meant every damn word I said about going to jail behind him, killing for him, any fucking thing. That shit was scary as hell because I didn't know if he loved me the same and worse than that I felt like I was losing a part of who I was.

Then on top of that shit, him almost dying made everything that much more real for me. Here we were about to have a fucking baby and he might die at any minute. The bitch coming over and popping off at the mouth sent me over the edge.

It was just too much. There were so many what ifs. I didn't know if I could take the heartbreak if shit when bad. Just hearing that there might be a possibility of him cheating on me crushed me. If you would have asked me months ago if I would give a fuck about a nigga fucking other hoes that I was with, I would have laughed at that shit. But none of them niggas had the damn key to my heart, to my damn soul. Saint was my everything. I would die for that nigga.

Jolie didn't get details from his ass at the dinner. But she was able to tell me how messed up his whole attitude was. He didn't even act like the usual brother she knew. He was quiet as hell and didn't respond when he heard the news about the baby. She said it was like he was distracted by other shit on his mind.

That was no good either in his line of work. I knew that the last thing a street nigga, let alone head of the organization itself needed were distractions. That shit got men killed. There was no room for it what so ever.

I decided to call Saint and see if he picked up. One of us needed to stop being stubborn. I didn't know if I wanted to chance the hurt that he could possibly cause me, but I knew being without him was torture. I swallowed my pride and hit the sent button.

He picked up after the third ring. There was a pause neither one of us said shit,

"Hey bae." I finally said.

"What's up?" Yeah he was real funny acting, his voice didn't show any emotion one way or the other.

"I just wanted to call and say I'm sorry. I'm so fucking sorry." I kept it at that.

Short and simple, but the truth. He didn't say shit at first.

"Say something. I mean it was all wrong, the whole damn fight, I'm sorry. Can we get past this? I love you." I continued since he wasn't saying shit.

"NyAsia, I'm cool. Right now I'm busy... You good? You need anything?" He changed the subject, not answering shit I just said.

He wasn't that damn busy if he answered in the first place. He was avoiding the conversation and avoiding me.

I was at a loss for words. This was the first time Saint ever held back from saying shit. He was treating me completely different than what I was used to. This shit hurt my feelings just that quick too.

"Nah, I'm good. Ummm, I got a couple days off before starting my new job. So can I come out and see you. I think we need to talk in person and get things settled." I said grasping at anything to get him to change his tune.

I knew seeing me face to face would force him to have this conversation and forgive me. I definitely wouldn't try and surprise his ass again. That shit went bad as hell.

"I don't think that's a good idea right now. Shit's pretty hot. I'll be back soon. Anything else, the baby good?" He tried to cut me off.

"I'm coming! So either you make the flight arrangements or I will. You can see for yourself how the baby and I are doing when I get there later." I said with determination.

I was serious as hell. I was going out to Houston with or without his permission. This avoiding shit wasn't about to fucking happen in our relationship. I knew I fucked up and hurt him. I was to blame, but he shouldn't have let a bitch suck his dick either. He wasn't all the way off the hook.

143

Now the other shit about me needing space, I was just talking out of fear in the heat of the moment. My head was clear and I knew what the fuck I wanted and that was my family. I wanted my nigga back and I wasn't taking no for an answer.

"Love you." I said then ended the call as quick as he tried to do.

A few minutes later a text came thought from Saint, not saying shit but with a link to my flight information in first class. Yeah, he was still gonna take care of me and make sure I was safe even on bad terms. Knowing he loved my ass still and just something small like setting the flight up caused a smile break out on my face.

I got up and got to packing right away. Terrell only had one more day before the weekend. He was turning 18 next week and more responsible each day. He would have the place to himself this weekend with the security team Saint left with him.

That was another thing I noticed over the last few days, there was a few niggas watching in the distance. I hadn't talked to Saint, but Drew called and let me know their names and showed me pictures of the three guards surrounding us. My man would do anything to protect me and our family.

I was gonna make everything up to him as soon as I touched down in Houston. He had no idea how sorry I was.

Saint

Nya was on some straight bullshit, talking about she was coming out to see me whether I said "no" or not. That was exactly the kind of shit a nigga like me couldn't put up with. With this street shit, I needed to know my bitch was solid and not so damn hard headed that she would put herself at risk.

She should be thinking about my damn son anyway. Nya thought she was off the hook by me taking care of the flight and shit, but her ass was gonna have to get in line with the shit when I talked to her.

I really wasn't trying to fuck with her right now at all since her mindset was all fucked up when she let that shit fly out of her mouth back home. Nya had my heart and was still my damn wife but I needed to do exactly what the fuck she asked and give her some space.

She had to either be in this shit all the way or get the fuck out. I wasn't with the going back and forth. I hoped I didn't misjudge her character and she could handle everything this life entailed.

I needed someone I could always count on, because there were always gonna be ups and downs. You couldn't bring in this much bread and live this amazing ass life without the hardships that came with being in the game. Anybody that thought otherwise was stupid as hell.

Being out here away from Nya for the time being allowed me focus on getting my operation in Htown straight. Another reason I had to keep a level head was to make sure I tracked down this pussy nigga I was looking for.

Before getting hit, I never even had a full opportunity to get things up and running out here. Now I was going hard as fuck to make sure both Houston and the West Bank were on lock.

With how strong my team was on the West Bank for so long and with the support of the three C's, I shouldn't even have to worry about mothafuckas back home. But Buck was gone and after Smoke's snake ass tried to take over, I didn't trust shit in New Orleans. I didn't trust the niggas on my team like I did my day one partna and that would never change.

Drew was the next closest man to me and had proved himself time and time again. He had stepped the fuck up out here in Houston and I didn't regret trusting him yet, so I planned to keep shit going how it was.

He was basically running everything on his own since the take-over. I needed to be back in New Orleans as soon as possible and couldn't stay out her permanently. It was just a gut feeling I had you could call it.

So I planned to show face and speak with some of the niggas Drew put in charge of the spots. Then let him do his thing. He wasn't under me anymore but more of a partner in this shit. I wanted to meet up with the niggas on our team only as a precaution and make sure there wasn't any funny shit happening. If some snake shit got past Drew, I wanted to weed it out of the niggas.

Drew was trusted by the crew and he was the only person I was even fucking with right now on the real. With the niggas who were behind the hit still at large, I was constantly looking over my shoulder.

Having two cities with big crews required me to make this decision. I was still technically the boss here, but Drew was the face for the most part, unless I needed to intervene. Drew deserved this opportunity plain and simple.

It spoke volumes when I told him about his promotion and ol' boy wasn't even trying to take the shit at first. He said he would rather I take control and let him continue to enforce shit. He was a little crazy in the head too. Shit, to work with me or right up under me you had to be. I didn't allow that pussy shit near me. Drew was a solid soldier, but he was meant to be bigger than that.

Thinking about my nigga Buck was fucking with me more these days. Like this shit we were dealing with right now.

I was waiting on Drew at our new private spot in Houston. A building that me and Buck thought up together before he was gunned down. While I was recovering he got the ball rolling and had the shit finished. That was my nigga.

The entire building was converted into a place equipped to handle problems. Whether it be another snake on the team or something to do with the product that required a secure location. We could do it all here without 12 breathing down our necks.

The old boss we took out had a different spot for handling shit but I wasn't about to put my shit at risk like that. Everything he did was over exposed.

Drew came back in the room pushing the nigga he brought with him in front to lead the way. The man's hands were tied behind his back and Drew held the back of his neck. The nigga looked young, probably not older than 20, and scared shitless. It was too bad he did some fucked up shit that led him here. But that was on him now.

Duct tape covered his mouth and his cheeks were tear stained. If a man was weak, that shit always came out when they were faced with the consequences of what they were doing. A solid ass nigga really built for this street shit stayed ready to die and still take what they knew to grave. Mothafuckas like that were hard to come by though.

After doing this shit for a long time, I had only come across a few that didn't blink an eye with the end coming. Drew stopped walking and released the man by the neck pushing him forward, then coming to stand next to me.

He pulled out a Newport and lit that bitch up, offering me one. I didn't smoke unless I was drinking so I shook my head and he put them back in his pocket.

"So what he do?" I asked Drew.

"Stealing out the same trap he's supposed to be working in. Taking your shit and then dumb enough to come back. This

149

mothafucka thought he was about to get always with the shit." Drew said inhaling a pull from the cigarette then letting it out in a cloud of smoke.

I shook my head back and forth. This nigga had to be dumb as hell to be trying to not only bite the hand that fed him, but really fucking with his own money by undercutting the other niggas around him. That shit was never good for business.

I walked over to where he stood in the middle of the concrete room. He had his chin to his chest. When I came up in front of him, I grabbed that shit and brought it up, to look him dead in the eyes. He couldn't escape facing shit head on with me.

I pulled the tape back from his mouth fast, but his ass still jumped like a bitch. This nigga should have never been on our team to begin with.

"Speak up nigga. Why did you take my shit?"

"I.... I... had to." He stuttered.

"What do you mean you had to?" Drew's interest piqued.

The nigga looked back and forth between me and Drew then back to Drew who asked the last question.

"I don't know, mane, some big time nigga from out of town wanted to sample the shit. He took my sister and said she was dead if I didn't bring him some of the shit. I didn't question him, I had no choice."

"What did he look like? You get a name?"

"Nah, I ain't see his face like that. It was dark as hell, but I did hear someone say his name. Julius. That was the nigga. He rolled up on me when I was walking home and got out of his car with two other niggas with him, pulling their heat. He gave me an hour to bring the shit back to him at the same spot. He showed me a video of my sister tied up to a bed. I didn't have a choice. I swear, mane."

I spoke up, "NO, you did have a choice, you could have come to us with this shit before you made the decision to take what didn't belong to you. If you would have done that, I would've gave you the dope and you would've got your sister back, believe that. Your team would ride for you, like you should have done for them. Instead, you're on some snake shit, coming against us. You might've done the shit for the right reason, but you fucked up lil' nigga."

I aimed my tool at his head.

"Wait, wait! He yelled out.

Looking frantic as hell. Sweat pouring down his face mixed with the old tears that had dried up. But his ass shouldn't be in the streets and definitely shouldn't have done some fucked up shit like he did. He did this shit to himself. I couldn't tolerate a nigga stealing up from under my fucking nose.

"I know where he's at. I met up with him the next day. He told me he was gonna cut me in on the bread from the shit I took for him. I didn't know why he did the shit, but I was gonna give YOU the money and tell you what happened. I swear mane, I swear. I put that shit on everything."

I almost laughed at this pitiful ass nigga begging and pleading in my face. He almost made me feel sorry for him for a minute. But then he just kept right on talking and now everything was clearer than before.

He was betrayed our team, whether pushed into it by that nigga Julius or not. This shit was in his blood. A man either was real or he was fake. Not only did he already sign his death warrant, now he just made me want to fuck him up before I offed his ass. He decided to keep fuckin' with the same nigga that made him rob me and took his sister.

"Where the fuck is he? I kept the shit trained on the nigga's head.

He paused, but then thought better than to delay the inevitable. "He's staying over in Gulfton. Look at my phone. It's all there."

Drew came up and pulled his phone out of his pocket.

"How do you unlock this shit." He barked orders to the nigga holding it up in his face.

"It's 1111". Damn this nigga was dumb as hell. He didn't even think of some shit for his damn password. I was looking at it like I was fortunate to find out sooner than later how fucked up in the head he was. To avoid the shit costing me or Drew more later.

Drew unlocked the phone then spent another minute going through messages and shit. He finally found what the fuck he was looking for and gave me a head nod indicating he had what he needed.

I already had some information on this nigga Julius from Juan. Him stealing and shit wasn't adding up. From what Juan told me, he was big time in Texas and out for blood since me and Nya offed his little brother.

It turned out that pussy nigga Jaquan, that Nya was fucking with and we got rid of, had a couple of older brothers who were in the streets. One was into some other shit besides drugs here in Houston and the other lived in San Antonio but had a small operation here along with other cities across the state.

I lowered the gun and threw a left hook connecting with the nigga's jaw. His face shot back from the impact. I stepped away, held the gun up and pulled the trigger.

He wasn't a bad worker before this according to Drew. Shit, he probably was telling the truth about his sister being taken too, but that shit didn't matter.

There was a street code to all this shit and for my organization to work and continue to profit, running like a well-oiled machine, I needed to stay on top of shit. This nigga deserved to die. He made choices and they were the wrong fucking ones.

After his body slumped over, I tucked my pistol in the back of my pants and let my shirt fall over it. It was time to call the cleanup crew.

The cleanup crew came and handled everything in under an hour. That's why these two niggas got fucking paid. They moved in silence and got shit done without a problem every time.

I read over the text Julius sent my worker a few times making sure there wasn't some kind of code with it. It seemed straight forward. Julius planned a meet up with him tomorrow.

Tomorrow, couldn't come fucking fast enough for me. I was so ready to get past this shit and kill this nigga. I instructed Drew to bring about 5 soldiers from our team that he trusted the most.

I still didn't know any of the mothafuckas that worked for me out here like that. And that shit worked in the end, especially now that Drew was gonna head up Houston. That meant a whole lot fucking more money on his end, more responsibility and more shit to deal with no question.

He would do just fine with it. I saw the hunger in his eyes, even if he didn't yet. His race didn't mean shit to me. A man was either about his money and was solid or not. All I got from him over the past year was loyalty and hustle. He knew how to boss the fuck up when needed. He was just the right amount of crazy to run shit.

When I left the spot, I headed home, until I remembered that Nya was supposed to be landing soon. I made a quick U-turn headed out to the airport instead. Her plane should be landing any minute. So I turned up my music and hit the highway.

Riding along listening to Jeezy got my head right. Not worrying about the shit tomorrow and definitely not thinking about this shit on the home front. Nya had my fucking heart, but she didn't deserve that shit right now. I wanted her to be my ride or die, my queen but maybe she was none of those things.

At first, I thought I was the one that wouldn't be able to do right by her, but now that I made shit official I was all the way in this bitch. She could be mad at me and make me earn her trust back for fucking up with the bitch when we first got together, but I needed her to stay by my side.

I would have given her all the time she needed because after that shit, I already knew I wouldn't be fucking up again. I didn't even look at other women anymore. But Nya was holding back. Then when I thought she was letting her guard down some, she tried backing out. It wasn't about the bitch sucking my dick either.

I wasn't about to do this kindergarten ass juvie shit with her. I was a grown ass man and a nigga that didn't put up with bitches to begin with. I thought Nya was different, but maybe she wasn't. Maybe I was just stuck on the idea of who I thought she was.

I pulled into the arrivals lane and drove slowly forward following the line of cars in front of me. I was driving my cocaine white BMW jeep and even though it was dark as hell with no stars or moon in sight, heads turned when my bitch rolled past.

A few minutes later when I was almost up to the main doors that led out from baggage claim, Nya sent me a text saying she

156

had landed already. I sent some simple shit back letting her know I was out here.

She came walking out of the automatic doors looking like the fucking queen I saw her as. I wished she saw what the fuck I did and realized how beautiful she was. Her confidence was another reason why she wouldn't let me love her right.

She was wearing some leggings and a crop top little ass shirt that read "Pink" across the shit. Right now, I was pissed off that she was wearing some shit like this out in public without me around. Even from where I was I could see her pussy print in the fluorescent light that shown down on the walkway.

She shouldn't be walking around like she was still single, just like her ass shouldn't have been showing out fighting that bitch Martina. She needed to get her fucking head on right and remember she was about to be somebody's mother now. All that childish and ratchet shit needed to be left in the past. After the baby, I didn't want her fighting and shit period.

If she was with me, she didn't need to do none of that shit. I wasn't just some corner boy and she wasn't just another hoe out here. She was hood royalty if she was with me. I was humble, but I wanted my bitch to be a fucking lady in these streets.

Looking at her more had my dick hard and head fucked up. I turned down the music that was helping me keep my cool the whole way here and that's when she spotted my ride.

She walked over towards it. When she got to the door, I thought about being petty and keeping that shit locked. But I wouldn't ever have her out here looking dumb. So I unlocked the shit and she slid in next to me with her one bag that she carried over her shoulder. She turned and placed it in the backseat, putting her sexy titties in my face.

She smelled like peaches and was rocking her natural hair, combed up into a puffy ass ponytail. Sporting the necklace and bracelet I got her the first day she officially moved in with me. The white gold and diamonds shined bright as hell contrasting against her dark skin. Damn, I was tempted to grip Nya's waist, lift her up and set her on my lap after I stripped her down, right the fuck here.

But, I wasn't about to do shit right now. To be real, when she told me she was coming out here, I would have rather she didn't and the main reason wasn't her safety. I really wasn't feeling her right now, no matter how much I loved her.

Maybe this shit wasn't gonna work and we were better off not being together and just raising our baby in separate households. I couldn't be worried about my bitch's loyalty daily and whether she was gonna bail on me.

I turned my head and ignored her, while she sat back down getting comfortable next to me. I saw her looking at me out of the corner of her eye, biting her bottom lip and all, showing she was nervous. Why the fuck she was nervous I didn't know.

"I'm sorry, I'm sorry, damn you know I love you though. Can't you forgive me?" She asked irritated, trying to flip shit.

Nya was too damn spoiled with me. With anybody else she wouldn't have tried to act like this. It was my fault. I gave in to her and Jolie too much. She was trying to play me for a fucking pushover.

But that shit wasn't gonna fucking work. I did that shit the last time when she acted like a hoe on my birthday and I gave in. I let shit slide and gave her the benefit of the doubt. Not this time.

"I ain't trying to hear shit right now." I said in the nicest way possible, but let her know I wasn't going for it.

I never talked to her how I talked to other bitches, but maybe I should have. Maybe she was just like the rest.

Her neck snapped around and the next thing I knew she was punching my shoulder and arm not as hard as she could but hard enough. I was forced to pull the car over to avoid running off the damn road. We barely made it out the damn airport parking lot without her trying to kill us out here. She didn't give a fuck about her, me, or the baby.

Once the car was stopped I grabbed both her wrists and held them bitches in a firm grasp. Her breathing was fast and she looked fucking crazy. Her chest heaved up and down and her eyes were full of fury.

"You're not 'bout to talk to me like I'm some fucking bitch off the street nigga. You know who I am, act like it! Damn! I don't' give a fuck how mad you are, you're not gone disrespect me. I will kill yo' ass before I let you do that shit. We're gonna get past this and you're gon' accept what the fuck I'm saying and take my apology."

She was crazy as fuck, if she thought she was gonna boss up on my ass and I was supposed to take that shit like a little ass boy.

"Nah, baby. You got the wrong one. You wanna do this shit here. Then fine, let's do this right fucking here." I stared back at her with the same cold stare she was giving me. "I didn't ask you to come out here, but I'm still the nigga who looked out for you and picked your ass up. Knowing I didn't want to be around you or talk to you. You're hardheaded and spoiled as fuck. Yeah I'm mad as hell. What the fuck you want Nya!!!! You want me to be your nigga, DONE!!!. You want me to love your ass, DONE! The minute you feel like you might get hurt in this shit, you walk away and bitch out. You think I'm gonna be with a weak woman?! I don't need a fucking woman, you wanted this shit remember. I gave it to you, but you can't be a real bitch and hold shit down. You're playing with fire shawty. Fuck all this bullshit, let's just end shit and keep it moving."

By this time, she was all out crying silently but letting that shit show, not trying to wipe away the tears or hide her hurt. Fuck it, she did this shit and came out here when she was the one who asked for time. I wasn't about to let my fucking woman run me and tell me what the fuck to do. She couldn't be iffy and in and out, while I was all the way out here for her.

That was the same shit that led to my pops chasing a bitch, losing his fucking mind and money behind it. Nah, that couldn't be me. I rather us go our separate ways right now.

"I said I'm sorry, I mean it. I love you. I don't want to lose you." She finally replied back calmer than before. But the fact was, everything I said was nothing but the damn truth. She didn't have shit to say back either.

She realized I was done talking about it. Until she could decide whether she was coming or going and really let me know what was good, I was cool on Nya.

I turned my head forward again, ready to get back on the road and get the hell home to my spot. But Nya reached over and placed her hand over mine on the steering wheel, moving her other one to my dick.

She found the mothafucka through my pants. Even with the arguing, my shit was still hard. I turned my gaze back on her and our eyes locked for a minute.

In that moment it was like we were speaking to each other. She might have been sorry but that didn't change shit about our situation. The physical connection and mental connection was the real thing, but she needed to grow the fuck up and decide if she could handle a man like me.

Nothing else was said, as she began stroking my dick through my jeans. I was still a nigga after all and she was still mine for life even if we were on bad terms. Wasn't no way I was gonna turn down my fucking pussy. I knew that bitch was leaking and Nya was ready to get some dick.

She leaned in for a kiss. I hesitated, but then thought "fuck it" and took control. I tongued her down rough and passionate, making us both more aroused.

Then reached out and cupped her titties, pinching her nipples through the thin fabric. Nya pulled back and brought that shit up over her head. Her see through bra let her dark chocolate skin show and even darker nipples peek through.

I pulled the bitch down and went to work sucking hard on each one while massaging them in my hands. Since getting her ass pregnant, her breasts had gotten big as fuck and seemed to keep growing. I loved that shit. I loved every inch of her body. I kissed my way down and placed a few on her stomach,

"Your daddy bout to be up in there lil' nigga." I said to her stomach. "Take that shit off." I lifted up my head and told Nya.

She obeyed and started stripping down until she was butt naked sitting on the leather passenger seat. We were in a jeep similar to the one I had back in New Orleans. I went ahead and got the same interior, just another model that was bigger to keep for when I was in town.

The shit had enough room to fuck up front instead of having to go to the back seat. It didn't have tinted windows yet, but I didn't give a fuck. Whether it was daylight or nighttime, in private or public, when I wanted to get some pussy that's just what the fuck I did.

Nya raised up on her seat, getting on her knees. I slid my pants down and my dick sprang out. My bitch bent down across the console, ass up and face down. Sliding her mouth over my dick nice and slow.

Since that night I flipped Nya upside down in 69, she became the only bitch who could let the mothafucka hit her tonsils and not choke. She opened wide and swirled her tongue, taking my dick in further. She reached down and juggled my balls lightly making my shit sensitive as hell.

"Eat the dick shawty. All the mothafucka." I pushed her head down more with one hand and reached my right hand over, slapping her ass hard. I ran my index finger up and down the crack of her ass back to her pussy. That caused her body to shake while she started humming on my dick. I knew Nya's body and she was about to cum just from sucking my dick.

I stopped playing with her ass and brought my other hand up to her head,

"Make it nasty." I commanded.

Nya moaned and got back to work going faster bobbing her head up and down. Really making it slopping. Spit dripping down all sides of my dick, with her grip working up and down each time her mouth moved up to the tip.

She kept the pace working her jaws and then all of the sudden deep throated my shit, like she had never done before. Then she really fucked up by closing the back of her throat more, "MMMM"

"Damn, hold up."

Her hard headed ass heard me. I wasn't trying to cum yet, but she switched shit up and released the grip her throat had on my dick and then started sucking hard on the top half making me lose fucking control. I slammed her face down taking control of her pace, gripping her neck and hair.

She took the shit like a champ. My cum shot out and Nya kept right on sucking until she got every drop.

Then she finally let up and lifted her head up, wiping her mouth and licking her fucking lips looking sexy as fuck.

"Your ass just can't listen." I rubbed my hand on the side of her cheek. She turned her head to my touch and kissed my hand.

"I wanted to taste you. Your cum tastes so fucking good, daddy." She answered.

I reached both hands over and lifted her up over the console to my side so she was straddling my lap just below my dick. With her fat ass up near the steering wheel.

I gripped that fat mothafucka, spread her wider by moving my legs apart and changing my grip to her waist. I lifted her up with her hands on my shoulders, titties in my face calling my fucking name, needing some attention.

But instead I watched as I slowly slid her down on my dick. Seeing her pussy swallow the big mothafucka inch by inch.

As soon as she was all the way down and my shit hit the base of her pussy, I felt the tight ass pressure of her muscles squeezing and clenching down. I began giving her slow short strokes, not even letting her move up and down the way she wanted to.

All the sudden she fought against my grip on her waist and began riding the dick. Going wild as hell.

"Yesssss, fuck me. Saint! I love your dick. I LOVE IT!!!!" She sang into the air.

I slapped her ass then palmed it helping her really feel what I working with in her damn stomach.

Her pussy was gushing and she already cummed, but her body all but froze before she raised up enough to squirt all on my dick and get some of my stomach wet.

"You love the dick, but do you love your nigga?!" I leaned in and whispered in her ear.

Not giving her a chance to say shit else back. I put my head back against the car seat and began moving her up and down by the hips, taking control. Breasts bouncing in my face slapping up and down, pussy looking sexy and fat as fuck.

"Oh my God!" Nya paused again, pussy leaking. Then tried a nice slow pace working her pussy on me. But I wasn't having that shit. I only went harder and rougher. She started this shit and now she was gonna handle the mothafuckin' dick. All of it.

When she came down again, I moved my hands to grip her breasts, "put that pussy on me girl."

I kissed her deep as fuck, biting her bottom lip, causing just enough pain with pleasure. Then I moved down to lightly bite her hard nipples.

When I did that shit, she screamed out and grabbed the back of my seat. Doing just like I told her ass. She came up off her knees and squatted with both feet planted on either side of me on the seat. Moving up and down faster, her juices coating my dick. Damn.

I kept my hands on her titties squeezing them while Nya went to work bouncing up and down, head thrown back taking it all. I stopped her from riding and began digging slow and deep.

My dick pulsed as my nut came to the tip. I made her sit all the way down and stay put, stretching her beyond what I knew could fit. She moaned again and looked me in the eyes, while cumming at the same time I filled her pussy up.

She kissed me on the jaw then raised up and got back over in her seat. I took off my t-shirt and handed it to her to wipe the cum from between her legs until we got back to my place and she could shower.

We both stayed silent the whole time while fixing our clothes. I left my shirt off and lit up the blunt that was already rolled, waiting for me in the ashtray.

Shit was awkward as fuck. This was the first time we didn't talk and shit after fucking. I was still pissed about her iffy ass and she knew that shit.

The sex was out of the fucking world. She handled my dick just like the mothafucka was meant for her. But was she really the right bitch for me. I was starting to wonder about that shit.

Tonya

It took me an hour just to drive the usual 20 minutes to my aunt Renae's house because traffic was a bitch and there was an accident. I hoped that Julius hadn't got in his brother's ear yet and Renae didn't hear shit about me taking off the way I did.

My aunt was all the way out there with most shit, but going against her nigga wasn't something she would ever do. For a long ass time now, she worshipped the fucking ground he walked on. It didn't help that he was a damn pimp and ran that same type of shit on her. Even though she wasn't technically hoeing for him. He had her turned out in other ways. Like being a damn pimp's assistant.

Some of the shit I witnessed this last month even made a heartless bitch like me cringe, and she did the shit without a trace of remorse. Selling young pussy to the highest bidder. She let some of the oldest grimiest niggas up in her home to get a quickie or an hour with a 12 or 13 year old.

She had two girls staying up under her roof getting raped on the daily, just for a place to fucking stay and food to eat. Not that they had a damn choice. Her nigga made sure to put fear in them if what Renae was doing wasn't enough to persuade them to play their role.

Not to mention the drugs they kept flowing in their systems. The heroine, pills, and powder mandatory to keep the girls going and making them money. The girls were actually pretty as hell and seemed like they probably had decent lives before getting mixed up with my aunt and her boyfriend.

I didn't ask how the shit happened. I didn't get involved in other people's shit. It wasn't my fucking business. This was just how shit went out there. It was a cold ass world.

I hurried up and ran into the house, going as fast as possible trying to locate Renae. She hardly ever left the house in case one of the hoes left while she was gone, so I found her sitting on the couch with the TV turned up loud as hell.

Even with the TV turned up you could still hear the loud thumping coming from the wall behind the couch where the headboard of the bed in the room was banging, probably from a nigga getting his nut.

"Why are you running in here. You better not be caught up in some bullshit you brought in my house." She was right, but I wasn't gonna let her know that shit.

171

"No, auntie..." I paused to catch my breath. "I just found the bitch. She's here, in town. I need your help."

I played it off just acting excited to catch up to Nya and not let the uneasiness from Julius being after me show.

"Damn, let's go get this bitch then." She answered smiling at me and standing up. "This nigga already paid, and both hoes are gonna be out of it for the night anyway."

My aunt was really coming through. We already talked shit over and it turned out she was the perfect person to come to with some shit like this. At first she asked if I just wanted to fuck with the girl and have her on the walk with her nigga's gang of hoes downtown.

He didn't only have a few girls here fucking for money, he kept rooms at a motel in the center of Houston with some bitches on his watch making money for him.

But I didn't want the bitch Nya to live, otherwise I would have took her up on the offer. I wanted her out of the way altogether, never to fucking show her face again.

When I went after something, I went all the way and got what the fuck I wanted. From the moment she saw me in the club that night she should have read my ass and saw shit for what it was.

172

The stupid bitch probably didn't think her nigga was like all the rest. Just hours before she was all cuddled up with him in VIP the night of his birthday, her so called nigga was digging my pussy out stretching my walls with his big ass dick.

Just thinking about that day, my pussy got wet. I still remembered everything about my time with Saint from the way he smelled, his voice and definitely his dick. No nigga ever had me sprung the way Kwame did.

I might have fucked up calling out his government the first time we linked up, but he would forgive me for that. I knew he could, because from the way he gave me the damn business he loved the way my pussy fit his shit too. He might've been mad, but that didn't stop the natural connection we shared.

I knew Saint felt the same shit I did. I caught him staring and eye fucking me whenever he saw me at the club after the shit went down. Now it was time to get shit popping and bury his bitch.

"Let's go."

Both of us were on the way out the door when my aunt's cell phone rang. She looked down at the phone in her hand, "hold up. Let me see what my baby wants."

She went to accept the call, but I slapped the phone right out her damn hand, causing it to fall to the floor.

I recovered quickly and shook the worry I felt, "What's wrong with you bitch, trying to get us caught up. No phone calls remember. Keep the lines dead. Wasn't you the one teaching me this shit? Just get up with him after, he'll be cool this one time. Help your family out, please." I prayed she didn't answer or call back.

She gave me a screwed up face but then nodded her head and picked her shit up.

"If I catch hell behind this, it's your ass. I ain't never made my nigga wait. But you're right, we got to be smart when it comes to this killing shit."

That was too fucking close. I swear sweat beads starting forming on my gotdamn forehead, but she didn't seem to notice.

Renae followed behind me and hopped in my ride without a trace of apprehension. It was finally time to put an end to this bitch and claim what the fuck was rightfully mine.

I was more than ready to become Saint's bitch. Soon it would be me on his arm instead of that ugly hoe.

Jolie

I found myself looking at my phone, staring down at the contact for Drew and scrolling though the messages and conversations we had since everything first went down. I was really missing his ass and wanted shit to get back to normal for us so I could have my friend back.

I still wasn't thinking anything past friendship. But he did mean something to me and not being able to share the shit that was going on in my life with him left me in a grumpy ass mood.

I wasn't really feeling talking to anybody more than I had to. Hanging with Nya these last few days was cool and things were getting better with her as well. But I still felt lonely as hell.

It was just me, myself and I at this point and that shit was probably how it would remain. Except I was gonna have a child.

Today was my monthly doctor's appointment and I was finally ready to find out the gender of what I was having. I didn't have any expectations one way or the other. Buck already had a little boy with his hoodrat ass baby mama.

Another thing I had been thinking about was how in the hell I was gonna end up making sure my baby had a relationship with his brother. Now that Buck was gone I had no idea how his son was doing.

The only reason his baby mama even halfway did the whole parenting shit, was because she feared what Buck would do if she didn't. She was an all-out hoe, who went out every weekend as much as possible dropping the baby off with Buck.

It had really been on my mind a lot lately to check in and get up with her to come to some kind of understanding. But my feelings were all fucked up and I put the shit off. I decided after the doctor's appointment, I was gonna swing by the place Buck had her staying at and see what was up.

I went ahead and put my phone down, thinking it better if I don't call Drew and just let shit be between us for now. He wanted more, and right now all I wanted and needed was a friend nothing more or less.

I left out of the house and made my way across town to the new doctor I would be seeing. After arriving at the doctor's office and waiting a good half hour to be called to the back, I started getting real anxious for no apparent reason.

So far Dr. Wright was the truth and she made sure to come in and speak with me before the exam to make me more comfortable. Being a teacher I had decent insurance but my brother wanted the best and gave me the money for anything I needed, the night I went to dinner with him. His bossy ass basically told me I didn't have a damn choice in the shit and that I better get up with the best doctor in New Orleans.

So the very next day I set up the appointment with Dr. Wright. All her reviews were five stars and the office was nice as hell. It was true that money could buy you good ass care. It was crazy how different this place was than the in network physician I went to on the first checkup I actually went to.

"Sweetie, are you ready to find out the gender of your blessing?" She came in the room asking with a contagious smile on her beautiful brown face.

"Yes, ma'am." I answered finally letting myself get excited.

"Lean back. I'm going to open your gown and we'll see the baby on this screen here." She pointed.

I still had my bra and panties on underneath, so I had no reason to be shy. I was naturally hesitant to show off my body even to doctors with the insecurities I had with my body. But I guess I had to get over that shit now that I was gonna be all the way exposed going through birth and shit.

I leaned back and the nurse assisted the doctor in putting the jelly substance on the end of the mechanism. The doctor proceeded to move it around over my stomach. She stopped when she got to the bottom right of my stomach.

"Well, it looks like you're having a girl! Congratulations! She looks healthy and strong already, good job mama." She finished taking measurements and then instructed me to sit and get dressed after leaving the room.

When she told me I was having a little girl, I was speechless. Tears welled in my eyes and I fought to control the emotions going through my mind. I was gonna really be somebody's mother and have a daughter.

This shit was surreal to me. I wish Buck was here. I pushed the thought of him away and finished getting dressed then picked up the few pictures the doctor printed for me, taking a minute to stare at each one. "My blessing" I thought thinking about what the doctor said. Wow.

I left the doctor's office finally feeling more at peace with my pregnancy and couldn't seem to stop touching my stomach, talking to my daughter as if she could hear and understand every damn word. We were in this shit together, things were gonna be okay. I was gonna make them okay for her.

I went ahead and headed over towards the apartment complex uptown where Buck's baby mama, Domonique stayed. It was time to bite the bullet and get this shit over with. I hated the thought of even talking to this dumb bitch and had done everything to avoid speaking to her trifling ass when Buck was still alive.

She didn't even know we were official, but always was on some petty ass shit when it came to me. It was like she knew I had his heart and she was the worst type of jealous bitch. She did the most to call him with some bullshit lies anytime we were kicking it or around each other even on the friend tip.

A few minutes later, I pulled into the complex. I found her apartment and made my way up to the top floor where hers was located. I knew exactly where the bitch lived. I had followed Buck here on a few occasions to see if he was still fucking her. There was only one time where he stayed a few hours and I knew he fucked her.

We had a big ass fight and I didn't talk to his ass for two months behind his doggish ways. I even went and fucked another nigga to piss him off. That just ended badly for the man I was with. Damn, we wasted so much time being childish. If I had only known that our time would be cut short...

I swallowed my pride and knocked on the door. This nasty bitch answered her luxury apartment door with nothing but some panties on with her titties out and all, hanging there like it was normal. I got a look behind her and the place was completely trashed.

I'm talking clothes, food and a stench coming from the place. I cringed and tried not to let my disgust show. I needed to try and make shit right the best I could.

"Bitch, what the fuck do you want?" She asked with the nasty attitude she always had.

"Look, I didn't come here to start no shit. Can we talk?" I asked and paused before saying anything else.

It was taking every in me not to check this girl. First of all I was trying to get shit settled and second, I was pregnant and didn't want to be out here fighting risking my baby's life.

Surprisingly, she moved to the side and let me in her apartment. I stepped over the piles of clothes scattered all around and thought about sitting down, but decided against it. It seriously looked like this bitch hadn't cleaned a thing in over a month. There were even dirty ass diapers all over the floor causing the whole apartment to smell, and making my stomach churn. It was starting to make me gag. It was that bad.

I wanted to hurry up and say what the fuck I came here to say.

"Where's BJ at?"

"Why does it matter to you where the bastards at?" She said catching me off guard.

I never held a conversation with Domonique, but heard her plenty of times playing the worried and concerned parent role whenever she wanted my nigga to come tend to some shit for her. Now she was acting like she didn't have a fucking child. I was starting to lose my patience. There was no way she would have said that shit if Buck was still living. This hoe was testing me.

"The fuck you mean? Where's your child, damn?"

"Don't worry 'bout what I got goin' on in my life hoe. You think your something special 'cus your brother. But bitch, I could care fucking less about that shit. Now Buck's gone you finally get the nerve to step to me. I will end your life hoe. Stop playing with me, yah heard." She said like she was all big and bad.

I swear after I said what the fuck I came here to say I was knocking her out and getting the fuck up outa here. This girl fucked with the wrong one. She should've heard about me.

I reached out and grabbed her by the throat clasping tight as hell. Her eyes got big as fuck and she tried to grasp at my hand with her fingers for me to let up. She struggled for a second, before I squeezed harder cutting off her damn air supply more.

She got the fucking message and stopped fighting against the hold I had on her.

"I ain't playing with your ass. You're gonna tell me where the fuck BJ's at and then I'm taking him with me. All that slick shit you were talking better be the last fucking time you come for me bitch. I'm taking BJ with me and away from your unfit ass. And if you try to do something about it, you'll be dead and I mean that shit on God! Get your life together and be a fucking parent. Don't come my way 'til you do." I pushed her back a few feet as I released her neck from my grip.

She coughed and leaned over trying to catch her breath. Then she looked up at me and gave me an evil ass look. She finally got some damn sense and went over to the couch picking up her robe and putting it on fast as hell though. All the sudden her ass was moving fast as fuck. When before, she didn't seem bothered by shit.

She was obviously strung out on who knows what. But I meant what I said, I was gonna take BJ with me and make sure he was good. No matter how I felt about Domonique I loved kids. That was why I became a teacher in the first place. More than that, I loved Buck and BJ was a part of him.

"Where is he?"

"In the room, I'll get him."

She went ahead and walked down the hall. I didn't trust her ass that much, so I reached in my purse and put my hand on my pistol, *betty*. I never left home without the bitch. Saint made sure I was official with my aim too. She better not try me or I would gladly use my friend.

A few minutes later Dominique came back with BJ walking behind her looking a mess and scared as hell. I had been around him a bunch of times, so as soon as he spotted me he took off running in my direction.

It really was sad as hell how pitiful he looked, wearing a dirty ass pamper and no other clothes. Looking like he hadn't seen a bath in who knows how long, hair a mess and still smiling ear to ear. He was innocent and this shit wasn't fair to him at all. He looked relieved even if he didn't know better.

"Hey lil' man. Say good bye to your mama, you coming to stay with me for a while. Tell her you love her."

I bent down and scooped him up in my arms despite how bad he smelled. He was almost identical to his daddy. I could only hope our daughter shared some kind of resemblance to the man I loved.

He turned and said, "Love you." As good as a three year old could then reached his arms around my neck and clung to me for dear life.

BJ spoke up right before I made it out the door, "See daddy?"

Hearing him ask for his daddy caused tears to well up again in my eyes but I held them back and shook my head.

"Nah, baby. It's just us and your little sister."

"No seeeester." He said adamantly.

"Yes you do now. In my belly."

He smiled and nodded his head. BJ always seemed smart for his age. His speech was still developing but he understood a lot more than he could speak on.

I turned back around and gave Domonique a look that let her know I meant what the fuck I said, every damn word. She had tears running down her face. I didn't know if it was because she realized how fucked up she had her son living, thinking about Buck or for the fact she just found out she wasn't the only bitch to have a baby by him now.

She never knew until today that I was with him for real. But I didn't give a fuck how she felt. She was a disgrace and BJ deserved better.

Nya

Me and Saint rode in silence the rest of the way to his place after the intimate sex we just shared. I hadn't been to his new penthouse apartment that he told me about yet. The last time I was out here it wasn't ready yet and only bad shit happened.

I couldn't even lie I was apprehensive to touch down after the last flight I caught. But I lived in Houston for a long ass time, so it was like my home away from home. I needed to come see about my man and get shit back right between us.

Even after hooking up, I was still feeling uncertain about where we stood. When he came at me with that fucking attitude I wanted to cry so bad. That shit hurt my heart to feel like he didn't give a fuck about me no more.

I loved him so much, too much. That was why I blew up and tried to make him give me some space after that hoe he was fucking with showed up at the house. It felt like a knife to the chest tearing me apart thinking about him cheating on me. It was a betrayal to do that shit to me.

He explained everything away and I believed his ass. But who was to say he wasn't gonna fuck up in the future. I needed to prepare my heart to take that fuck up if or when it came.

I was only weak behind Terrell for so many years. I made so many vows to myself that I would never be broke down like I was at the time I left my aunt's house, when those niggas were raping me.

Granted, it was a different kind of defeat. But Saint held the ability to break me down completely. I was scared of loving his ass too much. I went about shit all wrong and now he was doubting my feelings and whether I was down for him. He shouldn't doubt that shit though. I held him down when he was on his deathbed and would always be here for him.

He fucked up. I fucked up. Shit.

But he warned me after the first time, that this was lifetime love and I didn't have a way out. Where was all his talk now? He needed to understand where I was coming from. I was determined to make him understand.

He pulled up to the new apartments that were built last year. I had passed by these plenty of times on the way to work at the insurance company I used to work at. It was still shocking how things changed for me so fast. Now I was about to be staying in one with the love of my life.

I never wanted to forget where the fuck I came from or that even when I was down and out in the worst way, Saint still saw the real in me. He helped build me back up to who I really was.

We pulled into the parking spot up front, waiting for the valet to come out. This gave me déjà vu, from his birthday night when I fucked up.

I was gonna talk to him and really open up this time though. Then maybe he would understand where I was coming from and even though it wouldn't make up for me pushing him away, maybe he would be able to forgive me again and get over his doubts.

I knew Saint inside and out, and realized that when he asked if I loved him while were having sex, that I really did hurt him with wanting space.

He deserved better from me and I was gonna lay everything out there for him. Hopefully he wouldn't look at me any different after he found out the demons from my past.

I didn't try and say shit while we were getting out the car or while walking into the complex entrance. But I did cling to his fucking side and hold his hand like my life depended on it. I wasn't gonna give him an opportunity to push me away or give me the cold shoulder. We were gonna hash this shit out point blank period.

Saint greeted the doorman and the man at the desk in the corridor. We were taken up to the 10th floor where the man servicing the elevator let us off. This shit was some real luxury shit. Saint was living in the best apartments out here in Houston.

Of course he gave each person a nice ass tip. Damn when I was living out here I was trying to scrape up dollars to make rent. I guess I still had to get used to how much money my nigga had and accept that life really had changed.

I followed Saint inside his apartment which was almost then entire floor, shared only with two other apartments. His place was fully furnished all white and beige colors.

I went ahead and made myself comfortable after looking in the fridge and grabbing a bottle of water and some takeout leftovers I saw.

"This still good?"

"Yeah, shit's good, I got it last night. You better be feeding my damn baby too Nya." He said trying to call me out.

He knew I was a light eater, but I had been doing good eating for two. When he first found out I was pregnant, I swear this nigga went and ordered take out from two different restaurants, ordering multiple meals without even asking if I was hungry. He said, that I had to feed his son good shit so he came out a beast. I laughed at his ass, but did kill a lot of the food.

"I've been eating Saint! I ate a whole quesadilla and pancake meal for lunch, you ain't gotta worry. The baby is doing just fine, daddy." I answered and rubbed on my stomach.

Saint smiled at me and came over to where I was standing near the kitchen island. He leaned down, kissed my exposed stomach below where the croptop ended. I wasn't showing yet at only 2 months pregnant, but that didn't stop his ass from acting like I was.

I knew Saint was gonna be the best damn father. Shit his ass basically was a father his whole life taking care of Jolie and now taking care of me. It was just his nature to be a provider and protector.

He stood back up and then put some distance between us. His attitude changed up and his face went back to that cold blank stare he wore so well. Damn he was so good looking, my pussy was ready for another round already even though I was still sore form the way he tore my cat up in the car.

I decided to go ahead and ignore his stank ass attitude and just push through. To finally get all the shit off my chest that I had been holding onto. I walked over to one of the sitting areas where there was a surround couch and flat screen TV posted in front of. I kicked off my shoes and stretched out my legs on the couch, leaning back against one of the arms.

Saint followed suit but instead of sitting near me he went all the way to the other side and picked up the remote like he was just gonna turn on the TV. Like everything was normal even though we were on bad terms still. Fuck that.

"Uhh-uhhm," I faked coughed getting his attention. He paused and set the remote back down.

"What's up shawty, what else you got to say now?" Damn there goes that fucking attitude.

I ignored him again and persevered through, trying not to get emotional or nervous. I never cried so much in my life before getting pregnant. I was all the way out of character.

I looked down at my feet. "I never want you to think for one minute that I don't love you with everything in me. But you got to understand that this shit is hard for me. Loving you, loving me, all of it."

He started to say something, but I held my hand up so I could continue. I needed to tell him and then he could say what he wanted.

"My life changed so much when my parents died. I was forced to leave the people I loved. Jolie and You, the rest of my family. But I decided to just make the best of it and be the best big sister I could to Terrell. When we got out here, my aunt Renae had other plans than just raising us. She... She had this boyfriend, well he... he was a pimp or something. He would set it up where men would –"

"Those niggas are dead!" He raised his voice and stood up, looking frustrated.

I finally looked up and saw the rage written on his face. I held back the tears and went ahead continuing with what I was telling him.

"They would pay and then rape me. The first time, I tried so hard to fight him off. I kicked, punched all the shit I knew to do, but he was bigger and stronger. He ended up punching me, knocking me out and when I woke up there was blood and pain. After that, I became numb to all the shit and just survived, completely broken. I didn't love anything, not Terrell, not myself. I shut it all off. Then one day Terrell almost walked in on a nigga raping me and something in me snapped. I saw the pain and fear in his face and at that moment I knew I had to get out of there and make sure he didn't get hurt like I did. From that day on, I lived for him.

Everything I did. My heart was still cold to the world and every nigga in it except my little brother. Then you came back in my life and slowly I started to let you in. I love you so much Saint. So much it scares the fuck out of me. I can't lose you and I can't let you hurt me. I don't have it in me to be like other bitches and accept you cheating or doing me wrong. I might really go crazy behind the shit. I've been hurt too bad." I looked in his eyes intensely without crying but still with all the emotion I felt showing.

He nodded his head, "You ain't got to ever worry about that shit. I ain't like these other niggas either. You'll never feel that hurt again with me. I'm your nigga for life, shawty. You riding with me?" He finished with asking.

"'Til the mothafuckin' wheels fall off." I answered with a smile back on my face.

He came over to where I was sitting and sat down by my feet lifting them onto his lap. I felt his hard big ass dick sitting between my calves. He saw me looking at him and moved his hands up my leg and then brought them down the front of my stretch pants giving him easy access.

He started working his finger in and out around my clit, making my pussy slippery wet. I was already dripping reading for another session.

His phone started vibrating and he paused what he was doing to look at it. I recognized it as his business phone. He went ahead and answered and I immediately saw the irritation on his face.

"Yo.... Alright" He only said a couple words then hung up.

He set his phone down on the coffee table and lifted my legs back up resting them down again on the sofa.

I started to sit up but he bent down and kissed the top of my head.

"Nah, baby it's nothing. Just a package downstairs. I gotta sign for the shit. I'll be back in a minute. When I get back I'm eating the shit out of your pussy. I want you ready, waiting for your nigga."

I swear his words were like music to my ears. My pussy automatically purred ready for the promises he was making. His tongue game was the fucking truth and the way he made my body feel was out of this damn world.

He walked out of the front door and I hurriedly got my ass up and went in the big ass bathroom connected to his room that I found. I took the time to wash up some before he got back. Then got in position on the bed and spread my legs, rubbing on my clit, waiting for my nigga to get back and fulfill his promise.

I heard the door open just as I was starting to get into touching myself, making the juices flow more. I looked up into the doorway and gasped. Instead of Saint walking back in, I was completely caught off guard when the last bitch I expected to see walked in the room.

What the fuck was going on and where was Saint?

Saint

Some shit was off, as soon as I got downstairs, the staff was nowhere to fucking be found. This building was supposed to have 24 hour security. Not that they would be a match to come up against any niggas who were out to get me, but for them to just be gone, vanished sent off all the alarms in my head.

I turned around to get back on the elevator and hurry the fuck up getting back upstairs. I needed to make sure Nya was okay.

But when I looked back out the front entrance, that bitch I fucked back in New Orleans at my club, was standing there smiling at me. She was looking crazy as fuck. This was the first time when I saw her that she was wearing this kind of look on her face.

I knew her ass was off from the first and only time I fucked. I tucked that shit to the back of my mind at the time, but I guess you could never underestimate a crazy bitch. She must have been up to some bullshit.

After Nya confiding in my ass and finally fully opening up, I wasn't about to let this hoe that I wasn't even involved with fuck shit up for me. She was obviously out here for a fucking reason. Her ass was probably the damn reason why there wasn't any staff in sight.

She probably had some shit planned to make a scene. Or to come onto me in a way that it would look like we had something going on to Nya, even though we didn't.

I went to the door and threw that shit open, taking a step out then snatched the bitch by the arm. She only half struggled against me pulling her back into the building. After the door was closed I still held firm on her fucking arm.

"What the fuck are you on?"

"What do you mean?" She stumbled back a couple steps as I let go of her arm. Then regained her footing.

Standing in high ass heels and a short ass dress having her entire body all but exposed for no damn reason. I wasn't checking for her ass on any day. Definitely not with my bitch upstairs. She looked me in the eyes and said sweetly, "It's okay baby, I like it rough too. Don't you remember." She really took a step towards me like we had some shit going on.

This girl was out of her fucking mind. I hemmed her up again this time by the throat, squeezing just enough to scare her. But best believe if she tried some fuck shit like this again I was killing her ass. Nobody was gonna stalk me or come after my old lady with some bullshit. It was lights out for any mothafucka who tried to come against me or my family.

"Stop playing with me bitch, Get the fuck out of here. I don't know you. I don't fuck with you. You come around again, it will be the last fucking time, you heard meh."

I let go of her for a second time and then turned to walk away. She didn't come after me crying or throw a fit so she must have understood I was serious as hell. I got the fuck on the elevator headed back to my room.

Wasn't this some fucked up shit. Getting stalked by a hoe that I fucked one time, before I was even with Nya. Now I was having to deal with bullshit behind it. I was glad as hell I wasn't out here fucking with any other hoes any more. The drama that came with the shit wasn't worth it. Every fucking time it was some dumb shit.

I made it down to my door and walked inside the apartment. The place looked the same as I left it, but Nya wasn't in the living room anymore. It was quiet as fuck, and I got a bad feeling that some shit was off.

"Nya!" I called out.

No answer.

I went ahead and pulled my tool out and held it by my side walking faster with each step through every room. When I got to my bedroom, I noticed the top cover on the bed was all fucked up, like it was just slept in. My shit was always made and neat unless someone was in the bitch.

I went in the bathroom and saw a fresh used towel on the side of the sink. Nya must have washed up from the looks of it.

After making it through all the rooms and not seeing a trace of Nya, my stomach dropped. Nya wouldn't have just fucking walked out and walked away. I was downstairs in the front lobby the whole time, so there was no possible way she just left.

I went over to the balcony and looked down at the busy ass street below. Thankfully, she wasn't laying below on the pavement either. That meant that the bitch downstairs was just a fucking distraction to get at Nya and I fell for it like a fool.

The bitch was part of some bigger shit and some other mothafuckas must have come up here while I was downstairs and took Nya. That was probably how the hoe knew my government. She most likely was up to some shit the whole fucking time even back in New Orleans.

I called Nya's phone to see if by chance the shit was on her. I heard the buzzing and followed the sound until I was back in my bedroom. I bent down and picked the shit up from under my bed.

I had no fucking clues to go by now. But I needed to act fast before some shit happened to my fucking heart and my seed.

I would make the whole damn city bleed behind some shit fucking with them. The niggas out here didn't know who they were fucking with.

I went ahead and called Drew first then Juan. Juan was back in Puerto Rico since that was his main residence, but I let him know what the fuck was up. He said he would touch down out here tomorrow to help along with a team of niggas at my disposal.

"What's good." Drew answered casually.

"I need you to come by my spot, those pussy ass niggas got Nya."

"I'm on the way."

Click.

Drew was on his way over right the fuck away. That was why I fucked with him. He was solid as hell. No questions asked, he was down to ride like fucking family.

I went downstairs, waiting for Drew to pull up. I didn't know if that fuck nigga Julius had anything to do with this shit, but his ass was the most probable mothafucka in the city. So his ass was gonna help me get Nya back even if he wasn't responsible then he was dead. Instead of tomorrow that shit just got pushed up to tonight.

My gut was telling me that he had something to do with her disappearance anyway, so he better be ready for what was coming his way. I didn't care if it was 50 against 2. He was gonna die tonight.

Tonya

"What the fuck!!!!" I yelled out, feeling the shock of the impact from the SUV behind us slamming into the back of my car.

I already knew exactly who the fuck was in the car without even seeing the nigga.

"Bitch, what the fuck you got me involved in?" My aunt questioned copping an attitude.

"Now ya'll bitches 'bout to die. You thought he wouldn't come for me." The dumb hoe in the back spoke up being real fucking bold all the sudden.

She wasn't talking none of that shit when her ass was walking to the car with her hands handcuffed behind her back at gunpoint. My aunt really came through and held shit down back at Saint's apartment. Everything went according to the quick plan we threw together.

I was supposed to cause a distraction after we baited the doorman out of his post and scared the shit out of the young ass white boy with threatening his family while holding a gun to his head. That boy pissed himself and got in his car fast as hell headed home while we watched.

The shit was too fucking easy. Saint should have been way more alert for being such a big time drug dealer and all. He was really slipping when it came to his vulnerabilities.

While I was downstairs fake throwing a fit to distract my nigga, Renae used the back staircase used for emergencies to get Nya and bring her downstairs. By the time she made it downstairs the bitch was breathing heavy talking shit to me, but she still got the fucking job done.

Now we had the dumb hoe secured and were on our way to this spot Renae knew about on the outskirts of the city. Some wreckage yard or some shit. She didn't have an address and said it was off the damn map. It was cool with me.

Either way the bitch was about to die without a trace leading back to us. Renae assured me, we wouldn't even have to use our guns to shoot her, that the place would do all the work. I didn't ask any other questions.

"hah, hah" I laughed loud. "That ain't MY nigga Saint baby girl, that's another nigga trying to take your ass out. You really know how to make enemies bitch. I'll give you that."

"Fuck you!" She yelled.

Then she got real fucking courageous all the sudden and spit on me, with the shit landing on the back of my neck.

Since I was driving I couldn't hit the hoe, but my aunt did that shit for me. She put her gun on her lap and swung on her closed fist punching her two times in the face back to back. I couldn't really see how much damage her licks caused, but the bitch didn't say shit else after that.

It was too dark to see much in the backseat through the rearview mirror.

"Who the fuck is behind us Tonya!" My aunt was mad as hell yelling and demanding.

Before I could answer another car pulled out in front of us from the intersection we were getting ready pass through. The streets were pretty dead the further we got from the center of Houston. The damn car that pulled out, forced me to slam on the brakes coming to a complete stop.

I attempted to put the car in reverse to get around, but when I did, the SUV slammed back into the rear-end of our car.

"Fuck, Fuck" I slammed my hands against the steering wheel.

"You got me going against Julius and my nigga bitch. I'm gonna kill your ass myself." Renae leaned over and tried to grab at me.

I was too quick for her fat ass and hurried up and got out the car, slamming the door behind me.

Julius and his brother each got out of one of the vehicles that blocked us in. Julius came up from behind. I already knew it was him driving the SUV and his brother from the front.

I wasn't worried about my aunt's pimp ass boyfriend. I had no reason to be since he went and snatched her up out the car and threw her in his car rough as hell, slapping her before forcing her inside. Treating her just like he did all of his hoes.

Julius walked up behind me, standing only a few inches away. Chills went down my spine from his evil ass. I always loved the way this nigga fucked me and the sick ass side to him turned me on in the bedroom. But right now, he scared the fuck out of me and I hadn't even seen his face yet.

He wrapped his arm around my throat from behind and put me in some kind of fucking hold, cutting off all the air supply. I clawed at the hold he had on me, but my vision faded and everything turned black.

Before I lost consciousness I turned to the side and saw my aunt's boyfriend pulling Nya out the backseat. I gave her one last smile making sure she saw that even though I was in some shit, she was still going to die tonight.

She thought Saint was gonna come save her, but she was dead fucking wrong. At least Julius would kill her ass even if I couldn't finish what I started.

Jolie

I had called Drew three times in the last hour, finally giving in to my thoughts of wanting to talk to his ass and he didn't answer one time. I went ahead and sent a few texts back to back trying to get him to call me back.

Maybe he was with some bitch. I caught myself thinking about him more and more since he told me he had feelings for me. I couldn't help the shit, he had been there for me and we had grown so close the last few months.

There was still no way I was going to be with him. I couldn't move past the man I loved that quickly. But I realized with me thinking about him constantly and now feeling a little jealously about him possibly being with another woman, there were some feelings on my end too.

I tried to tell myself that it just wasn't meant for me to talk to him tonight since he wasn't answering, but then another thought came to mind. What if something was wrong? With the life he was in and having my brother in the streets just about my whole life, I knew firsthand the risks involved with being in the drug game. Enemies were always coming after those who were above them in status. It was just how shit went.

I called Drew one more time, and still no answer. I decided to call Nya and see if some shit was going down out in Houston, since I knew her ass was headed out that way to see Saint tonight. She sent me a text when she landed and made it to his apartment to let me know she was safe.

Even though we were just getting back to having our friendship on closer terms, knowing she was going out to see Saint again gave me flashbacks of the last time she did some shit like that, and everything snowballed afterwards.

To my surprise, it wasn't Nya that answered but my brother instead. I knew some shit was up the minute I heard his voice.

"Man, shit's bad right now."

"What happened, Oh my God? Is it Nya? Drew?' I asked getting more worked up.

"I'm taking care of it, believe that. I'll hit you up later. Watch out for lil' brudda and make sure shit's secure. Love you girl." He answered.

"Love you too." We ended the call.

I hurried the fuck up and went to check on Terrell and bring him back home with me. I also needed to go to the businesses Saint had and close them for the night. After he was hit up last time, he had run shit by me, Nya and Drew. When he said "secure" the shit, that meant I needed to make sure all his assets were secure.

There were safes at each business and he wanted the places closed so it would be harder for a mothafuckas to hit the spot and get away with the shit, since he had security on them. I was also headed back to my house because as smart as my brother was, his house didn't have a safe room like mine did.

That was just like his ass though. He insisted I have the shit, but didn't look out for himself. Of course his house was built before Nya came back and they got together. He never saw himself having a woman by his side until her. Now I bet his ass would have done some shit differently.

From what Saint told me, I still didn't know if Nya was in trouble or Drew. Shit, maybe nobody was in trouble and it was some other shit going on. I knew his ass wouldn't give more information over the phone in case it was tapped.

So all I could do was hold shit down for my big brother and wait for him to get back in contact with me.

On the way to pick up Terrell I made sure to drive about five over the speed limit but not too fast. I had no idea as to what threat my family was up against and the last thing I wanted was to end up delaying shit with a ticket. There were so many times when I was younger that Saint ran through countless scenarios to me about how to handle shit or act.

Even though my adrenalin was pumping, his words filled my head and I was able to keep my cool. On the way, I spoke a silent prayer to God.

"Dear Lord, please let my family be safe. Wrap your arms around Kwame, Nya,

the baby and Drew. Please God, in Jesus
name, Amen."

Nya

My mind was racing, trying to put shit together. The possibility that my aunt Renae came back into my life by accident seemed like too much of a fucking coincidence. But the look on her face when she saw me in Saint's room was straight up surprise like the same shit I felt.

The bitch continued to fuck with my life even when I thought the past was in the past. Having let everything out in the open for Saint to hear, relieved me of a lot of the pain and power the shit had over me. But not even a few minutes later, I was being confronted with it again. That made me feel like God was fucking with me too.

I tried to hurry the fuck up and get off the bed to find some type of weapon, but my aunt got the best of me with holding the gun trained at my head. She tossed a robe and a set of handcuffs at me. I kept my hands in the air, while I put the bitches on. I went willingly.

Normally, I would have put up a fight but I had to think about the baby now. I needed to stay alive and keep him safe.

When I was taken and raped before I had my blades on me, and the shit still happened. Now I didn't have any weapons and was helpless but I was still determined to

211

keep my head up and figure out a way to protect my unborn until Saint found me. I knew he would move hell and high water to find out where I was.

I smiled thinking of how that shit was gonna look when he came. I sat in the back seat of the car observing everything. There was another bitch driving. I had no clue where these bitches were taking me. But it looked like they were driving out of Houston and headed north.

I wasn't scary, and having a gun pointed at me, even now being handcuffed going wherever the fuck these two were taking me, didn't scare me one bit. Shit, I had already been through almost everything there was to go through.

I didn't want to let them know I was pregnant and made sure not to hold my stomach like I usually did. My evil ass aunt would end up punching or kicking me in the stomach on purpose to cause me to lose the baby. She was pure evil.

The minute the one driving opened her mouth, I recognized her as the same hoe from Saint's birthday. My aunt landed a few good punches, right before the car came to a quick stop. I had to use my legs to brace myself for the slamming of the brakes to avoid flying forward into the seat.

Both of them got out the car. Well the one hoe did that was driving and Renae was pulled out by the fucking devil himself. I couldn't even be happy to see him roughing her up because he was the last nigga I wanted to be around. Just looking at him made me feel sick to my stomach.

Luckily, it was the other nigga that came to my door and grasped ahold of my arm. He wasn't gentle, or rough just firm.

I didn't say shit or ask shit. He pulled me behind him and opened the back door to a big black SUV. I stepped in without contesting and sat my ass down. He closed the door behind me and got in the driver seat.

He turned around and looked me in the eyes intensely and grinned like a fucking jackal showing off his gold plates in front.

"It's good to see you again."

Chills ran though my body and I shook involuntarily. I was fuming, ready to kill this dirty ass nigga smiling in my face.

I recognized his voice. He was the exact same man that shot up Saint's room and raped me in the alley. I remembered his voice like I heard the shit yesterday.

"Fuck you." I said simply without too much emotion, just cold.

He started laughing and turned back around, putting the car in drive. The engine was still on since he never turned it off.

I tried to be as observant as possible looking at everything and soon realized we were headed back towards the center of the city. That meant Saint would have a better chance of tracking me down.

I wasn't looking for him to just come in and save the day though. I wanted to get at these mothafuckas too. I noticed the car my aunt's boyfriend drove followed behind us the whole way. More than likely both those bitches were in the car with his ass.

I started plotting, planning to somehow convince this man I needed to use the bathroom or some shit and then find a weapon. I didn't have my blades since I was naked underneath the robe I had on but there might be other things I could find when we got to where we were headed.

The nigga driving began talking again out of the blue, catching me off guard.

"I was gonna wait and make you really pay for the shit you did, but now that you fell in my fucking lap, your times up bitch."

I was confused why this man seemed to have it out for me so bad. I didn't know this nigga from the next, yet he was on one talking about making me pay. I kept my mouth shut and continued to listen. I didn't have shit to say to his ass anyway. My mouth might fuck around and make me lose any kind of chance I had of talking him into taking these handcuffs off.

"I don't even know what my brother saw in you. You're bad I guess for a dark hoe, but your pussy ain't nothing. If he only knew you was one of the little hoes Jamal had working back in the day, he would've never fucked with you."

I still sat there in silence. This nigga talked too damn much. He might have a lot of damn money from the looks of the expensive ride and the clothes he was wearing, but he was a bitch. I could tell a sorry ass man trying to be more than he was from a mile away.

He was just like all the other wannabees. Running his mouth. If his ass wanted me dead he should have done that shit already. Playing games and all that extra shit was something a woman would do. Normally, I would have said some shit back and talked shit, but I wanted to play my cards right.

Within about 15 minutes from looking at the clock on the front panel, he pulled down Capitol St. and parked across from an abandoned building. It had boarded up windows and was down the street from a parking deck. It was dark out, but plenty of people still around on the street. How this nigga thought he was gonna have me walk with his ass towards the place I already knew we were headed, was beyond me. I wasn't about to go with his ass with a street full of witnesses and not say shit to someone and ask for help, fuck that.

He must have known exactly what I was thinking. His ass may have talked too much but he wasn't unprepared. He reached down on the floor of the passenger seat. I watched him take his time shaking something then he pulled his hand up into view and even though the inside of the truck was dark, the interior lights still showed him moving his hand towards me while holding some kind of cloth.

I leaned back into the seat and started shaking my head back and forth, then scooted my ass over to passenger door on the opposite side of his ass in the front seat. He leaned all the way over, still coming closer. I panicked and tried to use my hands still behind my back to figure out how to unlock the fucking door and open it.

Whatever he had on that cloth was probably bad for me and definitely bad for the baby. I lifted my legs and kicked as hard as possible, swinging my legs wild,

"Fuck you! Get the fuck away from me, I'll kill you!" I spewed any and everything, kicking nonstop to keep him away.

He was bigger and stronger, acting like my kicks didn't do shit to him or phase him at all. He finally pressed his hand over my nose and mouth covering them completely with the cloth.

It smelled bitter, burning my nostrils. I turned my head to the side again, but it was no use. I became lightheaded. Then there was nothingness.

Saint

Drew pulled up to the front of some building that looked like nobody had been inside in a long ass time. Less than an hour passed since Nya had been taken but I couldn't find her fast enough. Her and my son were in danger so any mothafucka tied to the shit was gonna die tonight.

This nigga Julius didn't know that we were on to the little shit he had going on with the nigga on my team, or that he was already on his way to the swamp in pieces. That shit gave us an advantage and I hoped like hell it caused him to be reckless in the shit he had going on. If he didn't think I knew about his little spot, his ass would probably bring Nya here if he had her at all.

All I knew, is that bitch who worked at my club in New Orleans was in on the shit. Other than that I was going off a whole lot of fucking guesses. Drew got out of the car at the same time I opened my door, stepping out.

I had two tools on me, one in the back of my pants and one in my hand, fuck the witnesses on the streets. These mothafuckas didn't know me out here still. I was the unseen boss. But Drew wasn't pussy, he had his shit out anyway.

This part of town was close to downtown but a little further out than all the busy spots. We hurried up and walked to the side of the building. I came up to one of the boarded up doors. After looking at it, I saw that it moved on the hinge of a nail at the top, confirming that some mothafuckas were here recently.

Drew took up my back as I moved the board to the side and stepped inside, keeping my steps as quiet as possible. After letting the board fall back into place we were engulfed in complete darkness. I stood there for a second trying to regain my senses and listened for some kind of sound to let me know where the fuck I was or who else might be in this bitch.

It smelled old like mildew, but as my eyes adjusted I was able to see a few feet in front of me. So I slowly took a couple more steps forward keeping my piece out, pointed at nothing in front of me. I didn't want to take my phone out yet and send off a warning to the niggas if they were close by. There was still no trace of light anywhere.

I stopped when I heard what sounded like footsteps coming from right above us. The shit was hard to make out exactly what the hell it was since the sound was muffled through the concrete.

I pulled out my phone so I could see now that I knew the mothafuckas were above us, not around us. There was a stairway about ten feet in front of where me and Drew were. We walked over towards it and then started on our way up.

I didn't know how many niggas were in the building besides us, but it didn't fucking matter. Nya was all that mattered to me. Life, death all that shit was out of sight out of mind.

Before we got to the second story we heard voices, so I put my phone back in my pocket real fucking quick and me and Drew both leaned against the cement wall on the stairway.

"What the hell you bring the bitches here for?" some nigga asked sounding mad as fuck.

"You know that's my bottom bitch, mane. She good. The other one's your problem."

"What the fuck was that back there then? She's good, but you can't control your hoe! She better not bring no heat my way nigga. After I make this bitch pay for good, I'm still handling her. Don't worry about the other one, it's lights out for her too. This shit tonight should open your fucking eyes, little brother, bitches ain't shit. Get her under fucking control."

The two pussy ass niggas finished talking and started walking in the opposite direction. Just like some hoes to be talking instead of getting shit done. Not my bitch though, she wasn't even about all that talking and playing around bullshit.

Now was our chance. Without talking shit over I made my move and ran up the last few steps. Drew followed behind still having my back. I aimed in front of me and began shooting even though the light was still dim as fuck, not knowing if I was hitting either one of the niggas.

It got brighter around us as the entire room lit up once we were all the way inside the main area of the second floor. This nigga had shit set up like an office, club and murdering spot all in one fucking area. It didn't even make sense how he had it laid out.

The nigga he was talking to was on the floor laid out. Drew stayed back a couple seconds and let off a few more to make sure he stayed that way.

This other bitch ass nigga was exactly who I was looking for. Julius was supposed to be the nigga in charge of San Antonio, but right now his ass looked like a bitch. He ran over to a large ass crate in the corner of the room and hurried up, opening the shit.

I stopped walking but kept my gun pointed at his fucking dome. He pulled Nya up out of the crate and held her in his arms. She was unconscious and handcuffed. Her entire body was fucking limp.

The sight of the woman I loved being out of it held by this mothafucka made me wanna kill the nigga a hundred times. I already knew he was the one behind me getting shot up and the shit that happened to Nya. Now he was holding my fucking heart.

"Drop the gun on the fucking floor." He yelled out. I dropped my shit on the floor immediately, but still kept walking forward.

I was gonna get as close to this pussy as possible. Then when I saw the opportunity I was gonna make a move. He side shuffled over to the big ass desk on the same side of the room and dropped Nya on the top of it, causing a loud thud and making me clench my fists at my sides.

I swear I was ready to kill this nigga. He aimed his gun at me, but his eyes moved to the side real quick noticing Drew coming up behind me. That quick second game me enough time. I lunged forward closing the distance between where I stood and where he was behind the desk. I heard two shots fire one from behind me and the other from Julius.

I felt a burning tear through my left arm as I slammed into this fuck nigga. His body already limp form the bullet Drew let off, that hit him square in the fucking eyes. Drew saw the shit the way I did, the minute he lost his focus, we took our chance.

I caught myself before falling all the way down where Julius' body already laid. I stood back up and snatched his ass up dead and all. Then laid blow after blow on his already dead body.

I was mad as fuck that I didn't get to torture this nigga or get the kill. But Drew did the right fucking thing. There wasn't no playing around when it came to Nya.

Thinking of her, my mind slowed down and I let go of Julius' bitch ass, throwing him back on the floor where the fuck he belonged. I stepped over to see about Nya and figure out what the hell was wrong with her.

I lifted her head gently off the desk and held it with one hand, moving my other all around trying to feel for some kind of lump or cut that made her unconscious. There was nothing. I shook her slow at first but then tried talking shit and raising my voice. Nya never could resist telling my ass off.

It was like she couldn't hear shit and she wasn't waking up.

"Nya! You gotta wake up, wake the fuck up shawty." I repeated really getting fucking worried. I scooped her up and her body was like dead weight making me want to spaz the fuck out.

"She needs to get to a fucking hospital. I don't know what the fuck that nigga did to her. Ain't no telling. Shit, she's got a pulse but it's real slow." I told Drew as fast as possible before walking towards the stairs.

Drew held his flashlight on his phone up to give us light on the way down. Walking as fast as possible we made our way out the door. Nya cradled in my arms.

"Damn, bruh she's gonna be good" Drew tried to reassure me once we were in the car and he put that shit in drive. He stepped on the gas, flooring the bitch driving well over a hundred on the all but abandoned city streets. At least there was no traffic.

Nya needed to be straight. Her and my seed. This shit had me on edge more than I ever felt in my life. I was a street nigga. I didn't fear death or none of the shit that might happen to me. But with my fucking family that was another story.

We were almost to the hospital only about a minute away.

"Fuck!' Drew hollered out of nowhere.

I looked up from having my head down in deep thought only to see fucking police sirens, red and blue in the rear view mirror reflected. I turned my head.

"Don't stop, let 'em follow us, she's gotta make it." I told him.

I didn't give a fuck about the pigs right now. I would take a hundred charges if it meant my wife was good. I dropped my gun at the warehouse anyway. Our cleanup crew could pick it up later. I didn't know if Drew was clean or he still had his shit, but fuck a charge this shit was life or death.

Drew stepped on the pedal, pushing it to the damn floor again and turned down the road that led to the hospital. As we made the sharp ass turn to the emergency entrance, I heard a few shots let off.

The car lost control and Drew slammed on the brakes causing us to spin around in a doughnut until we came to a complete stop. The impact caused him to hit his head on the steering wheel, but I was still alert. I jumped out the fucking car mad as fuck.

What kind of shit was this? It was obvious we were on the way to the fucking hospital, the mothafuckas shouldn't have stopped us and damn sure not fucking shot out our tires like they did. What the fuck was this?

"We gotta get my wife to the hospital!" I yelled out coming up to the side of the squad car and pounding on the shit.

The officer in the driver seat stepped out not saying shit. He came over to where I was standing in my fucking face.

"Hands up! Put them on the hood" He shouted trying to sound like he ran shit. Bitch ass police.

I put my hands up.

"Look, I'm just trying to save her life. We gotta get her there. Take me to jail after I don't give a fuck. But she's messed up. You got an obligation to make sure she lives, you heard meh." I was heated.

None of how this shit was playing out made sense. I was trying to talk sense into the crooked ass cops that I hated with a fucking passion. Right now, this shit might mean life or death for Nya so I swallowed my pride and all but begged this fucking man to do right.

The passenger door of the police car opened and I turned my head looking at the other officer coming out, gauging the situation. Maybe this mothafucka would hear some damn sense.

As soon as I saw who the fuck stepped out I tried to turn back to Drew's whip and make a run for it. It was too fucking late. The first cop slammed his button into the side of my head back to back. I went after him and got my hands around his neck, despite being beaten.

He clawed at my hands trying to make me release my grip that was robbing him of the air he needed to breathe, but I squeezed harder. These weren't fucking cops, well none that I was gonna listen to.

The mothafukca that came out of the passenger side came up behind me and wrapped his arm around my neck making me take my hands off the man I was strangling. That was all it took for the police officer in front to regain his composure and put his taser on me.

Still after getting shocked I tried to fight the two of them off. After another blow from behind to the temple I lost balance and my vision blurred.

Fuck, Drew was my only hope now.

"Wake the fuck up!" I managed to yell out as loud as possible before falling into complete darkens. Nya was the only face I saw come across my closed eyelids before my mind went blank.

To be continued...

EL Griffin Books

Gangsta Love Series

A Gangsta's Pledge
A Gangsta's Pledge 2
A Gangsta's Pledge 3 *coming September 2018*

Hood Love and Loyalty Series complete series

Hood Love and Loyalty
Hood Love and Loyalty 2
Hood Love and Loyalty 3

Made in the USA
Coppell, TX
09 February 2021

50004821R00135